PATSY KELLY INVESTIGATES

End of the Line

We'd been going for a couple of miles when the police cars started to pass us. Billy had turned the music up loudly so we didn't hear them at first. It was me who saw their blue lights blinking frantically behind us, moving rapidly alongside us, then in front. We watched them speed off ahead, the flashing lights becoming smaller, like blue bulbs on a distant Christmas tree. Then they disappeared.

When we got back to my house my mum had the news on.

"They've found a fourth body," she said. "Near the carriage bays, down the railway works."

Four bodies.

In ten days.

A Family Affair

Look out for:

No Through Road

P●INT CRIME

PATSY KELLY INVESTIGATES

End of the Line

Anne Cassidy

■SCHOLASTIC

Scholastic Children's Books
Commonwealth House
1–19 New Oxford Street, London WC1A 1NU
a division of Scholastic Ltd
London ~ New York ~ Toronto ~ Sydney ~ Auckland

First published by Scholastic Ltd, 1996

Copyright © Anne Cassidy, 1996

ISBN 0 590 13345 4

Typeset by TW Typesetting, Midsomer Norton, Avon

Printed by Cox & Wyman Ltd, Reading, Berks.

10 9 8 7 6 5 4 3 2 1

Contents

1
The Railway Children

They found the second body in the old disused track down by the industrial estate.

Like the first, she was fifteen and had been strangled.

It was Christmas Eve and Billy and I had been walking along by the river when the police cars had started going by; first one, then another, then two or three more. There was a sense of determination about the way they passed us, not speeding but fast enough to create a whoosh of air, and we stopped to watch them, the policeman in the last one less calm than the others, shouting something at the driver.

The road was eerily silent as well, an absence of sirens, just the sound of the wheels on the ground and a couple of kids across the way playing football; *pass it*, *pass it*, they shouted.

"That's typical," Billy had said, "when you're waiting for one they never come and then there's five of them together."

"OK," I'd said, "that's an original joke."

We followed the direction they'd been heading and saw them parked at odd angles just outside the old factory estate. Officers were going in and coming out and talking into their radios. They were shouting to each other and reversing their cars up the road to make room for a small unmarked van that had quietly crept down the street. A few minutes later we saw two men carry a long wooden box out of the back of it.

A policeman came towards us, pulling at the collar of his shirt as though it was too tight, and said:

"Off you go, be off home now. There's nothing here for you to see."

Billy whispered "Morgan's Hump" and I followed him off round the corner and up an incline.

We stood on the humpback bridge that passed over the railway sidings, unused now for many years.

Some of the lines were still in place, giant weeds growing up through the tracks. Many of the sleepers were missing, stolen probably, and there were two old carriages which sat, slowly crumbling, at each side of the yard. One line went straight into a long building and it was there that the police were.

"It's a body," I said, stating the obvious.

"On Christmas Eve," Billy said, under his breath, as if that made it more sad. Maybe it did, for the family; unopened presents and a decorated tree that would sit incongruously in the corner beside the cards of sympathy lined up on the mantelpiece.

We stood in silence for a while and watched, some kids and shoppers joining us. One man was carrying a huge Christmas tree under his arm and a number of heavy carrier bags. He let the tree rest against the side of the bridge while he stood and looked at the movements in and out of the siding.

An unmarked car slid along the side of a track. All the policemen turned and looked at it.

"I wonder who that is," Billy said.

The man with the tree and the bags of presents said:

"Well, it's not Father Christmas, that's for sure."

My uncle Tony had closed the agency earlier that day. He'd bought me a small present that he said wasn't my *real* Christmas present; he and my aunt Geraldine would bring that when they came round for Christmas dinner.

I couldn't wait.

I opened the small present while he was standing there. It was a Parker pen.

"It's an office present," he said, adjusting the knot of a new tie he had bought. "My thanks for the good work you've done here, especially since ... since..."

3

He meant since the Judy Hurst case but he didn't say it. I'd tried to find the murderer of a girl that I'd known at school. I'd almost been badly hurt in the process. Since then my uncle had kept his eye on me and I hadn't done anything more strenuous than answering two phones at once.

He'd promised to let me help him on a case though, after I'd made a complete recovery. I'd reminded him of it a number of times and he'd nodded seriously, as though he regretted what he'd said.

"Tony, about that case; the one I'm going to help with."

I left the sentence in mid-air, and watched as he combed his hair in the mirror. He cupped his hands and breathed into them. Then he took out a packet of mints from his pocket and absent-mindedly offered me one.

"The case, Tony. The one you said I could help with."

My words were like an echo and he looked momentarily annoyed.

"Your mum doesn't want you to get involved in that side of the business. Look what happened last time."

"But we did agree," I kept my voice quiet, calm. In my hand I rolled the Parker pen back and forward as though it were a cigar, "that I wasn't just going to work here as a clerk. You promised you'd teach me some of the skills of an investigative agency. That way, you said, I was less likely to get into any trouble!"

"Did I say that exactly?" Tony was packing up his bag, ready to lock up the office.

"Yes, more or less," I said. It had been more like: *we'll see, we'll see*; that famous adult phrase that meant *no, but I don't want an argument right now.*

Tony looked at his watch.

"Are you meeting Aunt Geraldine?" I asked.

"Yes," he said, looking irritated. She was taking him shopping and I knew he didn't want to go. He had planned to meet some of his ex-colleagues from the local police station for a pre-Christmas drink.

He looked at his watch and sighed.

"After Christmas, I'm looking into this insurance claim. A Mr Black who is suing the company he worked for because of a back injury. He says he can't work again, etc., etc. My job is to follow him for a couple of days and see if I can get a photo of him bending over. The company have had some kind of anonymous tip-off that he's faking it. Some nice friend he's got."

I listened to every word, trying to see what there was for me. I'd imagined being allowed to help in an important investigation; after all, I'd not done so badly in the Judy Hurst case. I'd pictured myself with a trench coat billowing over my DMs, dark glasses, maybe even a Trilby. I had one in my wardrobe at home...

"So what we'll do is this. You can come with me while I follow him on the first day and then on the second day you can follow him yourself. It'll be a good chance for you to get to know how to use a camera and surveillance techniques."

He picked up his bag and zipped it shut. He said: "See you about twelve, Christmas day."

He stood for a minute uncertainly, then he turned and went out of the door. I'd thought, for an awful moment, that he'd been waiting for me to give him a goodbye kiss. That he'd regressed some dozen or so years in our relationship to the time when the inevitable words came from my mum's mouth: *Give your uncle Tony a kiss now, there's a good girl.*

I was going to follow someone to try and catch them bending over. It was hardly big time. I felt as though I'd just had some scraps thrown at me and I didn't like it.

I turned off the lights in the office, even the little plastic Christmas tree. I closed the door and looked for a moment at the boldly painted sign: ANTHONY HAMER INVESTIGATIONS INC.

I turned the key, making sure that I had double-locked it, and went out into the street.

They found the third body the day after Boxing Day. It was in a station house that had been closed a couple of years before. Not enough people using the train, a waste of public money, British Rail said.

Like the other two, she was fifteen and had been strangled.

It was all over the national papers. They coined the phrase, THE RAILWAY CHILDREN, and everybody started to talk about the Railway Killer.

"It's a serial killer," my mum's friend Sheila said. "Apparently he leaves the scene of crime exactly the same every time. Strangles them with a piece of climbing rope."

"Honestly, Sheila!" my mum said.

Sheila had recently started working at my mum's college and she had a morbid interest in matters to do with death or murder. She was always reading books about crime or death: *Unsolved Murders of the Nineteenth Century*, or *The Mind of the Killer*, or some such stuff.

"I don't want to think about those awful details," my mum said.

"Do you think your brother, Tony, the detective, might get the case?"

"I don't think so," my mum said, casting a stern eye in my direction, a kind of warning look, as though I might go out and try and find the killer myself. "The case will be top priority with the police. My Tony only follows up things that the police have given up on, or personal matters. He mostly works for insurance companies."

"What about Patsy?"

"Certainly not. Patsy is just working as a clerk, to

give herself some pocket money for when she goes to university next year."

I said nothing. Sheila looked disappointed. She bit into a mince tart and my mum continued:

"I just hope the police catch him, before he does it to anyone else."

Sheila nodded her head but her eyes were staring into the distance, probably imagining the Railway Killer stalking the tracks; his victims soon into double figures. I thought, for a moment, I saw the ghost of a smile on her lips.

A couple of days later I took a drive with Billy. I hadn't seen him since Christmas Day when he'd had dinner with us. It was something he'd done for the previous couple of years, ever since his parents had died.

We were best friends, Billy and I, a bit more than that sometimes. He'd been busy before Christmas though and I hadn't seen much of him. Over Christmas we'd pulled a few crackers and eaten a lot of chocolates. He'd bought me a hat for my collection; a dark brown boater, with a mustard sash on it. It was even in a proper hat box. I'd given him a couple of kisses, one on each cheek. I'd only paused between them for a micro-second, the idea that I should kiss him on the lips only there fleetingly. Then it was gone and I'd stood back and tried the hat on again.

I'd given him a new shirt and a book about vintage cars.

He came round for me at about eight. I got into his latest car and closed the door. I had to pull hard on the handle because the catch was broken.

"That door's definitely coming off tomorrow," Billy said, "and I'm respraying next week. Metallic grey, you reckon? Maybe," he said; then gave me a quick smile before moving off up the road.

Whenever Billy and I met we didn't bother with chit-chat. We often just picked up the conversation where we'd left it the previous time. We'd known each other too long for niceties.

"Where are we going?" I asked, glad to be away from the house. The mince tarts and the turkey now brought on a mild nausea and the glitter of the tree seemed tiresome and garish.

"A bit of a drive? Then a drink?"

We'd been going for a couple of miles when the police cars started to pass us. Billy had turned the music up loudly so we didn't hear them at first. It was me who saw their blue lights blinking frantically behind us, moving rapidly alongside us, then in front. We watched them speed off ahead, the flashing lights becoming smaller, like blue bulbs on a distant Christmas tree. Then they disappeared.

When we got back to my house my mum had the news on.

"They've found a fourth body," she said. "Near

the carriage bays, down at the railway works."

Four bodies.

In ten days.

2
Surveillance

" *Serial killers.*" My uncle Tony said the words sarcastically. "They weren't called *serial killers* in my day. That's an American invention."

We were sitting in his car watching a terraced house a hundred or so metres down the street. Mr Black had not come out yet. We'd been there over an hour. On the back seat was a lightweight camera with a zoom lens.

"There was none of this morbid public interest either. You found a couple of bodies, you went on with the investigation, you caught the killer. There were none of these greasy journalists skulking around. Now every Tom, Dick and Harry thinks they can investigate," he said, his voice dropping. "What they don't realize is that detective work is mostly boring, mundane stuff. It's not all car chases and glamorous women…"

I wondered, for a moment, if any of it were car chases and glamorous women. I thought of my uncle's car. A five-year-old Ford that didn't always start; stretch tartan covers and a toy tortoise on the dashboard that was really an undercover air-freshener. I took a sideways look at my uncle; forty-five years old, ex-policeman, family man, immaculately dressed every day, mostly by my aunt Geraldine. I couldn't see many glamorous women in his life.

"Here he is," Tony's voice broke into my thoughts.

A man came out of the door and walked, slowly, to his garden gate and out into the street.

"Come on," Tony said, and we got out of the car. "We'll walk separately to start off. You in front for ten minutes or so, then you drop back and I'll take over."

I pulled my woolly hat over my ears and walked on. Up ahead, Mr Black was walking steadily. He went to the newsagent's and bought a paper; then to the library and chose some books. After that he went to the café where he sat over four cups of something and read his paper and part of one of his books. I had a cup of tea and sat for as long as I could without being noticed. Then I went out and my uncle went in and did the same.

I stood in a shop doorway across the road and waited for them to come out. I was starving but I couldn't go and get any food in case they both moved and I missed them. I was cold as well, my toes like hard pebbles at the tip of my boots.

I saw a headline in a newspaper hoarding across the street: RAILWAY CHILDREN: SCHOOL LINK?

It had been over a week since the fourth body had been discovered. All railway land, used and unused, was being patrolled, guarded, locked up. The dead girls had been named: Mary Williams, Kate Hargreaves, Sarah Roberts and Lucy Jefferson. They were bright achievers, high–flyers; the kind of kids that ended up at university.

Each day the newspapers had printed their pictures. Small, square school photographs that showed the top part of their uniforms; a shirt, a tie, a cardigan or jumper. Pale skin and no make-up; toothy smiles, a glint of fun in their eyes, their friends no doubt larking about behind the photographer.

It was one of the reasons why my mum would never buy any of the school photos that I brought home, year after year. She said they made her shiver, they reminded her of dead children.

There was movement in the shop. Mr Black was getting up and walking out. I joined my uncle and we followed him together, as though we were a father and daughter, out for a walk on a January afternoon. The camera was still over my uncle's shoulder, covered partly by a woolly scarf that he had hanging there.

Mr Black went back into his house and we sat and waited.

"I'll give it to about three-thirty. If he doesn't come out again, we'll call it a day."

My uncle was looking at a magazine, *Sailing Today*. Every now and then I could hear him mumbling "um, um," in agreement with something that he was reading. I put my head back on to the headrest and kept my eyes on the terraced house where Mr Black lived. After a while I felt my eyelids drooping and I had to make myself sit up in case I fell asleep.

I looked at my watch; there was still another hour to go. My stomach had stopped rumbling, but now felt as though it had caved in. More than anything, I wanted to get out of the car and go home.

What had I hoped for? To be part of an important investigation? Like the hunt for the murderer of the Railway Children?

In the distance I heard a train chugging by and wondered how the police were following up the case. I thought about Heather Warren, the CID officer who'd helped me with the Judy Hurst case; she had advised me to join the police, had said that that was where I should go if I wanted to be a *real* detective. Was she in charge of the investigation?

The fourth body had been found near the railway works, where the carriages used to be refurbished and cleaned up. Lucy Jefferson, fifteen, in her last year of secondary school. She'd been found fully dressed with a piece of climbing rope around her neck.

I tried to picture what had happened. Had she been walking along, approached by this man and drawn into a conversation with him? Had he asked her for directions somewhere? Perhaps said he was from out of town. *I'll show you the way*, she might have said. And then, while walking past railway land, had he overpowered her, pulled her back into some undergrowth?

I felt as though I was going to shiver but I didn't. Then I heard a sound; a low growling noise, rhythmic and slow. I looked round.

My uncle Tony's head had fallen to the side and his face was flat against the driver's window, his mouth open. His eyes were closed and his magazine had fallen on to his lap.

He had been so engrossed in the case he had fallen asleep.

Back at the office Tony gave me my instructions for the next day.

"Mr Black is due at the insurer's at eleven, so at least there'll be no hanging around his street. I want you to wait outside from about twelve onwards. You'll see him come out and then you should start to follow him. Give it a couple of hours. Here's the camera. It's an automatic, very expensive. You just point it. It adjusts itself and then, if you press this twice, very quickly, it will photograph half a dozen shots in quick succession."

I took the camera. It felt solid and important in my hand.

"Remember," my uncle said, "if you think he's seen you, just come back. It's no big deal. I have a feeling anyway that Mr Black is genuine. It's no skin off my nose. I still get paid."

When I got home, I put the camera by the side of my bed. I sorted out the clothes I was going to wear. A long coat with a hood; some heavy tights and a long pleated skirt. A close-fitting felt hat and a long scarf.

Somehow, the tedium of the afternoon had disappeared and I was feeling a jittery excitement about the next day. I was to be on my own; trusted with the camera. It was a bit like being allowed to walk home from school by myself for the first time.

It wasn't as though I was being given a case of my own, but it was a start.

3
Smile Please

In the end I wore some trousers and a zip-up jacket. I had a woolly beret on that I managed to pull down over my ears. It was still bitterly cold though and I stamped my feet and hugged my hands as I stood waiting for Mr Black to come out of the insurance offices.

In my shoulder bag I had the camera carefully cushioned and ready to be pulled out at a moment's notice in case Mr Black bent over. I also had a cheese and tomato sandwich that I'd slung together just before leaving home.

Mr Black emerged from the building at about twelve. He drew a sigh as he stood outside the main doors, and then took a look up and down the street. I was only a few metres away from him and I was able to see him up close for the first time. He was about fifty. His hair was thin and he had a small beard, just on the centre of his chin. He had glasses on and I noticed that the left arm had been fixed to the main frame with some black tape. He spent a minute delving into a deep pocket of his coat, then pulled out a handkerchief and loudly blew his nose.

I suddenly felt sorry for him.

I looked back into the foyer of the insurance company's offices. It was a forest of small pot plants and leather seats. On the reception desk was a huge bowl of flowers: lilies, roses, chrysanths, freesias; all the expensive, out of season, blooms.

My uncle had said that Mr Black had strained his back while moving some office furniture. He was making a hefty claim for injury and loss of earnings.

I wondered what a "hefty claim" meant. Tens of thousands? A few thousand?

Mr Black walked off towards the shops and I followed about twenty metres behind. I didn't feel particularly heroic. Some little man was trying to get a few thousand out of a huge company; here I was surreptitiously following him, for an amount that the company probably spent on its foyer pot plants every year.

It was David against Goliath.

Mr Black went into the same café that he had used the previous day. I took my beret off, put my glasses on, and followed him in. I bought a doughnut and a cup of tea and sat in the far corner. I got out a book and laid it open on the table.

He didn't notice me: he didn't even flick his eyes in my direction. He seemed preoccupied. After a while he got some small change out of his pocket and started to count it out on the table. I was beginning to feel such sympathy for him that I considered paying for his lunch myself.

I looked at my watch, it was one-twenty. A woman and a small child came into the café and Mr Black immediately stood up. The woman walked across to him, manoeuvring a pushchair in between the tables. He reached out and took the child, a small boy of about two or three.

"Hello, Dad," I could hear her saying, "another cup?"

"No, love, I've just this minute got this one."

Mr Black sat the small boy on his lap and started to talk to him using a lower, more gentle, voice.

"Where've you been then? To the shops? Have you got some shopping with Mummy?"

The little boy reached across him towards the salt and pepper pot on the table and said:

"Ganggad, Ganggad. Bin the sops, Ganggad."

I looked at my book and wondered how long the family lunch would go on. I sneaked one half of my sandwich out of my bag and stole bites from it, wary of the woman behind the counter noticing me. I needn't have worried though. She was gazing out through the window of the shop into the streets beyond, her fingers toying with a chain that was round her neck. Her lips were mouthing words from a song that I could barely hear from a tiny transistor radio on the counter.

Mr Black's daughter left at about two o'clock. Before she went she took out a bag and unpacked it on to the table. There was a plastic cup, a packet of baby wipes, tissues, and some food stuff that I couldn't quite make out.

"Are you sure you'll be all right?" she said, before she went.

"'Course I will. I'm only going to walk him down the park. *Won't we, my boy?*" Mr Black said, holding up a biscuit for his grandson.

The park was a small, square courtyard in the middle of a shopping precinct. It was like a tiny school playground with swings, climbing frames and a sandpit. There were benches round the side and I took a newspaper out of my bag and sat down to read. After a minute of the biting cold I took out a brown woolly scarf and wrapped it around my neck until it came up almost as far as my nose.

I wondered how long Mr Black would keep the child out in that weather.

I looked around. There were about half a dozen shops that were still open; two or three others that had been boarded up. Near me was a shop called

Ray's Car Spares that took up two shopfronts. Next to it was an Asian shop that had wooden boxes of fruit and vegetables outside and a sign that said: *videos for rent or sale*. An Asian woman came out of the doorway and scooped up some vegetables into a bag. Her sari blew romantically back in the wind and revealed her bare arms and midriff. I felt colder just looking at her.

I looked round at Mr Black. He was sitting on the edge of the sandpit while his grandson was playing. Now and then I could hear his voice: *Now we don't put that in our mouths, do we, son?*

Behind him, sitting on a bench, was the only other person in the tiny park. A teenage girl who was sitting staring into space, her hands in her pockets, chewing slowly.

I turned back and looked at the dry cleaner's that boasted "two hour service" and "expert alterations". The windows looked steamed up and a woman with a grey overall was looking out. I hoped she wasn't noticing me. The Chinese take-away next door had a notice that said "fish and chips, fresh every day" and I actually began to taste the salt and vinegar in my mouth. A packet of hot chips and a ketchup sachet would warm me up nicely. I even began to reach into my bag for the money.

A cry broke into my thoughts though and when I turned round Mr Black's grandson had fallen over. The little boy's mouth was wide open and a pitiful wail came out. The voice was fierce and full of temper and he seemed to be blaming his grandad, the sand, the air, even his own limbs, for the fall.

My first instinct was to get up and go over to help, but then I remembered why I was there. I watched for a minute as Mr Black stood helplessly looking at his grandson.

Then he bent over.

Everything in my head said no but I still got the camera out of my bag and positioned it. Click, it sounded; click, click, click, click, click, it continued to take shots automatically. Holding the camera and letting it take its own photos, one after the other, it didn't really seem as if it was me. I had just started the process off.

Mr Black had stood up by this time and his grandchild was seated in his pushchair.

I quickly stuffed the camera back into my shoulder bag and he turned to face me. His face was riven with pain, his mouth in a grimace and his teeth clenched. I watched with anguish inside my chest. I went to get the camera out again, but it was too late. He turned back, took hold of the pushchair and walked off.

I had missed a chance to photograph his pain. All I had got was him bending over. Exactly what the insurance company wanted.

I looked hopelessly round the tiny park. The only person who was there was the teenager that I had seen earlier. Her head was down though and she seemed to be digging at something on the bench beside her. She hadn't even noticed that the child had fallen over.

I shook my head; then I remembered that I hadn't helped either. I had been too busy doing my job.

I zipped up my bag and walked off towards the High Street.

By the time I'd got to PHOTOKWIK I'd decided what to do. The film had to be developed because there were other things on it that my uncle needed. I would pick up the snaps in the morning on my way to work and destroy the ones of Mr Black. I could say that I'd just taken a few practice ones at home and that I hadn't had to take any of Mr Black because he hadn't bent over.

That would be the end of that.

Feeling pleased with myself I gave the film to Larry, the man in the shop, and went home. My mum's friend Sheila was there drinking tea.

"Guess what," she said, "they've caught the Railway Killer. In the act!"

"Yes?" I said, still disgruntled about the afternoon, not really in the mood for one of Sheila's macabre conversations.

"Quickest police work I've ever seen," she said, "it'll probably be on the local news."

She turned the telly on and there, on the screen,

was Heather Warren, the policewoman that I had got to know on the Judy Hurst case. She was outside the local police station surrounded by reporters.

"Detective Inspector Warren, can you tell us about the latest developments in the 'Railway Children' case?"

Heather Warren was looking down at a piece of paper.

"I have a statement to read out," she said, and then coughed briefly.

"A man was arrested at approximately two-thirty this afternoon in the vicinity of the East London train depot. That man is now helping us with our enquiries. Any further developments we will share with you, if and when they occur."

A cacophony of voices erupted from the reporters but Heather Warren, looking away from the camera, said, "That will be all, gentlemen," and walked off into the police station.

Two-thirty.

Heather Warren had been arresting the Railway Killer at exactly the same time that I was photographing poor Mr Black.

"What do you think of that!" Sheila said, looking from me to my mum, obviously wanting to talk about the murderer and his victims.

"I'm going upstairs," I said moodily.

4
Caught!

I left home early and went straight to PHOTO-KWIK.

My mum had been for her morning run and I'd left her sitting, still in her jogging trousers and sweatshirt, watching Breakfast TV. I'd had to say goodbye twice because she was so immersed in the revelations about the Railway Killer. If her friend Sheila had been there she would have distanced herself and pretended she wasn't interested.

I got to the lab just after eight. It didn't open to the public until eight-thirty but Larry had said it was all right for me to come early. A young dark-haired man in a white coat came out of the swing doors. He was carrying a pile of envelopes and when he saw me he looked momentarily annoyed.

"We're not open yet," he said, dumping the envelopes on to the counter.

"Where's Larry?" I said, rather more brusquely than I meant to.

"Out collecting some supplies. Who's asking?" he said adopting a tiny smile and then letting it drop.

"I'm here from Tony Hamer's," I said, avoiding his direct look. "I'm picking up some film Larry said he'd have done for me." I was looking at my watch, trying to give the impression that I had a busy schedule. In fact I had very little to do that morning; some filing and some phoning around for payment. I wanted the photos though, in my hand. I needed to get rid of the ones of Mr Black; then I could relax.

"And you are?" he asked unruffled.

"Patsy – Pat Kelly. I work with Mr Hamer. These photographs – it really is quite an urgent job. I'm sure Larry has done them. He wouldn't forget a job for us." I was drumming my fingers on the counter top, aware of the young man's penetrating stare.

"Brian," he said. "Brian Martin, at your service."

"Right," I said. "Brian, any chance of looking for the photos? Just as a favour?" That's when I gave him a smile.

"That's nice," he said. "You've got a nice smile."

I gasped at this display of cheek. I stood in silence for a moment and looked him over. He had black hair and dark eyes. He was a bit taller than me and quite chunky. Underneath the white coat he had a dark T-shirt on with some writing that I couldn't read.

"Don't patronize me," I said dismissively. "Whether you like my smile or not I'd like you to go and look for the photos that Larry has put by for me. Otherwise, my company will be looking for some other photographic facility to use." My hand was trembling and my throat was dry but I kept my stare directly at him.

He didn't flinch. He smiled and said, "Certainly. Please take a seat and I'll see what I can do."

He disappeared behind the door and I sat down. The cheek of it! To be leered at so obviously; *to my face!*

I waited, fuming, for what seemed like hours. Only five minutes had passed though and I looked mournfully at the swing doors. They stood still, no tremor of movement that might suggest footsteps coming this way. The young man, Brian, had gone away with no intention of coming back. Perhaps I shouldn't have been so supercilious with him. Maybe I should have just continued smiling and got my photos by being nice to him.

I would just have to sit and wait. I picked up my bag and pulled my newspaper out and started to read.

The capture of the Railway Killer was all over the front page.

The police got a lucky break yesterday when a local resident spotted a man loitering around the East London train depot. After a quick phone call had been made to the emergency services, police raced to the scene just off Regency Road. A police helicopter was called, but in the event was not needed.

The man was apprehended while moving around the carriage bays. When the police found him he reportedly fled and ran along the tracks towards central London. He was chased and caught by officers and then informed of his rights.

The man has been named as 48-year-old Leslie Knight from Essex, a retired railway ticket inspector. Former colleagues are said to be "deeply shocked" by the arrest.

At a press conference late last night, the detective in charge of the investigation, Heather Warren, said that the man had been found with certain suspicious articles on his person, which, in the present circumstances — four dead teenagers — needed to be explained. It is believed that among these items was a length of climbing rope.

Mr Knight is due to appear at East London magistrates court this morning. It is expected that he will be held on remand until all investigations are completed.

The funerals of two of the victims, Mary Williams and Kate Hargreaves, are due to take place this week. The families will be relieved that the investigation has borne fruit so quickly. The bodies of the other two victims, Sarah Roberts and Lucy Jefferson, have not yet been released.

The noise of footsteps made me look up. The young man, Brian, had returned. He was not sullen as I'd expected him to be. He was flushed, quite jovial.

"Here we are!" he said. "Finally found them in Larry's tray. He had done them."

"Great," I said, giving him a real smile, and was momentarily flustered when his fingers touched mine as he was handing over the photos.

"So you're a private investigator, are you?" he said, giving me the invoice to sign.

"Yes, sort of," I said. He was leaning on the counter, nodding as though he wanted me to go on. I was keen to look at the photos though. "I must be off; thanks for finding the photos." I turned away.

"I'll tell you what – " I could hear his voice as I went out of the shop doors – "you can follow me any time…"

I repressed an urge to turn round and give him a mouthful. I tucked the photos away and headed back to the office.

As soon as I got to the office I sat down at my desk and sorted through the pictures.

Most of them were Tony's. There were several of a burnt-out shop and a couple of two men talking in a park. I wondered which case it was. There was even a photo of Geraldine, Tony's wife. It looked like the first photo in the reel, so perhaps Tony had been trying out the film.

The photo showed my aunt Geraldine in her kitchen, standing beside her Aga cooker. She had an apron on and in her hand was a spatula. She was pointing it at the person behind the camera and she had a half-moon smile on her face. At the bottom of the photo was the time and date that the shot had been taken: 11.49 a.m. 01.01. New Year's Day. Maybe something Tony had said to her had made her laugh. I tried to imagine my uncle Tony being witty or humorous. It didn't work. It was a bit like when I was a kid trying to imagine my mum and dad in a passionate embrace.

I put those photos to the side and laid out the six that I had taken of Mr Black. I sat down in my chair, my coat still on, and looked over my handiwork.

I'm not sure exactly what I had expected. Probably something that looked like a series of stills from a film. A slow-motion scene from the park. Mr Black looking at his grandson lying on the ground; two or three of Mr Black in the course of bending down; Mr Black scooping up his grandson and then Mr Black standing upright again.

The photos were quite different though. Firstly, they were all at a peculiar angle. They showed a slanted world and the top corner of Mr Black's back. I must have been holding the camera crookedly. Not only that but two of the photos didn't show Mr Black at all. He had ducked below the lens at that point and all I'd captured was a shot of the sullen teenager who'd been sitting on the park bench behind him. The most depressing thing was that none of the photos showed any identifiable bit of Mr Black. It could have been anybody.

I sat back, annoyed. I had wanted to throw the photos away anyway but it would have been gratifying if they had at least come out properly; if I had been able to manage the camera more efficiently.

Not only could I not identify Mr Black, but I had even missed him out. I picked up the two photos that he had dropped out of. I had a lovely view of the teenager sitting on the bench. She had her hands in her pocket and her legs splayed and was staring straight ahead, as though she was looking at something to the right of me. Her expression was one of boredom and I could even remember her slowly chewing gum and not even noticing when Mr Black's grandson started to cry.

At the bottom of the photo was the time and the date: 2.32 p.m. 10.01.

The exact time that the serial killer was caught.

It was just as well that Heather Warren did her job a bit more competently than I'd done mine.

I had a last look at the kiddies' park, the top of Mr Black's shoulder and the sullen teenager staring moodily at the world. She looked about thirteen. 2.32. Half past two, she should have been in school. Then I cut the negatives away from the others and put them, along with the photos, into the sink, and set light to the lot.

They curled and blackened and magically seemed to disappear, leaving a residue of what looked like black petals lying in the sink. I gathered them up and pushed them down to the bottom of the bin, underneath the tea bags and the empty biscuit packets.

I finished my tea and resolved to learn how to use the camera properly. Then I got out the forms and began to write out my report.

When I got home that evening and turned on the telly, I saw Heather Warren's face again. She was in the middle of a crowd of reporters. I could see two or three furry mikes being thrust at her and at first I didn't quite catch what the question was. The answer was clear though.

"The body of a fifteen-year-old white girl was found this afternoon. It was in one of the cargo bays in the Holding Warehouses, just adjacent to the

Regent's Road depot. The area hadn't been searched yesterday because there appeared to be no need. When the suspect was apprehended it was strongly believed that a further crime had been prevented. At that time we had no way of knowing that a fifth murder had in fact happened, perhaps only minutes before.

"Naturally, my officers are devastated by this find." Heather Warren turned abruptly away from the cameras even though there was a chorus of cries.

They had found a fifth body.

Five girls he had killed. The fifth one only minutes before Leslie Knight had been caught.

I picked up the remote and pressed the button. The picture died and I sat there for some minutes, feeling flat and aimless.

5

A Familiar Face

My mum was out with her friend Sheila so I watched the ten o'clock news on my own.

It was the same depressing story. During a routine operation two rail workers had stumbled on the body of a fifteen-year-old in a warehouse in a yard along the way from the Regency Road depot. The killer, widely assumed to be Leslie Knight, had done his work and was moving *away* from the scene of the crime; not *towards* it, as had been earlier thought.

Leslie Knight, having already been charged with the other murders, would now have to go back to the magistrates court to be charged with this fifth one.

The picture of the dead girl flashed on to the screen. It was another school photo, taken recently. She had a dark uniform on and her shoulder-length hair blended into her sweater. She was smiling, but only just, her lips upturned at each corner; no teeth, no dimples.

She looked familiar; but then school photographs often made me think of my own school and all the kids I knew then. She was pale with dark hair, not unlike any dozen or so girls whose pictures I had stored at the very edges of my memory.

Her name was Helen Driscoll and she had come from The Valentines, an estate bordering on a local park. "Estate" was the wrong word; it conjured up images of row upon row of identical houses punctuated by tower blocks and waste ground. It made me think of burnt-out cars and graffiti; unemployed teenagers parading with their outlawed pit-bulls.

The Valentines was a *private* estate of a couple of dozen big houses. It was a turning off a side road that bordered the park. The road was gravel and had several "NO ENTRY" signs posted along it. I'd been with Billy when he'd delivered a car that he had sold to a couple who lived down there. It was a small yellow mini that Billy had bought as a wreck and then painstakingly done up. The couple had wanted it as a surprise birthday present for their daughter. When we'd given it over to them the mother had rushed into her house and come out with a giant blue ribbon that she'd promptly tied round the car, as though it was a huge parcel.

Helen Driscoll had lived in one of those big houses.

And now she was dead.

The newscaster was reading the rest of the news, so I clicked the set off.

The house was strangely quiet without my mum being there. I looked around the room and saw her books and papers all over the dining-room table. Over by the door was a pair of her running shoes and draped around a chair was a jacket that she had worn to work that day but not got round to hanging up.

I suddenly felt very alone and wondered what my dad was doing.

He and my mum had lived apart for years. I saw him regularly but he often moved around the country with his job. I knew that he'd been in Birmingham for the last couple of weeks and I was tempted to ring him on his mobile. I even walked casually out to the phone in the hall and let my fingers drum lightly around the buttons.

What would I say though? *Hi, Dad, I'm feeling a bit depressed about these murders…*

Just then the phone rang and made me jump. I picked it up and said: "Hello?"

"That was quick," a male voice said.

"Yes?"

"It's me, Brian Martin. From PHOTOKWIK, remember?"

I stood with my forehead wrinkled up and let the name go through my head a few times. Brian Martin, Brian Martin.

"I'm sorry," I said. The word PHOTOKWIK flashed on and off like a neon inside my head. Brian Martin: the kid with the poor chat-up line.

"I'm the helpful young man who found your photos this morning."

"Right. Brian, how are you?" It was a stupid thing to say but it just came out.

"Good, good," he said, as if it had been weeks since he'd seen me. "We got off to a bad start this morning, Patsy. I was wondering if we couldn't get to know each other a bit, say go out for a drink, or a meal, or both?"

I wasn't sure I liked the way he'd put himself on immediate first-name terms with me.

"Where did you get my phone number?"

"Tony Hamer gave it to me," he said.

Thanks a lot.

"It's a nice idea," I said, "but I'm really busy at the moment." I could hear the key scraping on the lock and looking round saw my mum come through the door. She gave me a silent wave and went into the living room.

"Is this the brush-off, Patsy?" he asked.

The brush-off. Where did he get his dialogue from; an old film?

"I really must go."

"Patsy," he said, "don't turn me down!"

His familiarity with my name was beginning to annoy me.

"Goodbye, Brian," I said, returning the address.

I put the phone down quickly and leant on it for a minute, as though I wasn't quite sure that the voice had really been cut off.

"Who was that?" I could hear my mum's voice from the front room.

"Some kid," I said, not elaborating.

"Billy?"

"No, just some kid who I met today."

"Where?"

"In this photo lab Tony uses. He's just someone I met, nothing important."

I went into the living room. My mum was lying on the ground. Then she started her sit-ups.

"He?" she said and exhaled quickly. I couldn't see her face. I knew that her eyebrows were raised.

"Never mind, it's nobody."

"Are you going out with him?" she said in between breaths.

"No, I'm not," I said, laughing.

"I could lend you that silk top of mine." I could hear her voice as I went up the stairs, and I rolled my eyes.

After I'd got changed into my night clothes I sat on a chair and looked in the mirror for a while. At the right-hand corner my mum had stuck a sprig of mistletoe. It made me think of silly Brian and his terrible chat-up line. *You've got a nice smile*, he'd said.

I had an ordinary face, not unpleasant to look at,

but not the sort of face that sticks out in a crowd. My eyes were quite big and I had an average nose and uniform lips. Any description of me would sound like that of dozens of other girls of my age. I was five foot six and my weight wavered a few pounds here and there but mostly stayed around nine stone. Sometimes I could get my jeans done up and sometimes I couldn't.

My hair was longish; at least I was always growing it, but it seemed to have stopped at my shoulders. All in all, I was a bit of a shop dummy with glasses on. The only way I ever stood out was if I dressed myself up, made up my face or wore one of my many hats.

Billy always commented if I got dressed up: *I like that top*, or, *your hair looks good like that*. The previous week, when we'd been window-shopping in the Exchange, he'd said: *you'd look brilliant in that dress*, pointing at some long chiffon number in an expensive French shop window.

I'd felt a fizz in my chest when he'd said it, as though I'd actually been wearing the dress there and then and he'd been standing back, looking me up and down. For minutes afterwards I'd felt a mild shiver around my shoulders and couldn't look straight at him. I'd felt *embarrassed* to look at him.

Sitting there, in front of my mirror, I pictured Billy's face and remembered the time he had kissed me under the mistletoe, over a year before. It had been a long kiss and we'd jumped apart when my mum had come through the front door. My lips had been wet and I'd wiped them with the ends of my fingers. Or maybe I'd just put my hand there to hide the kiss, as though I'd imagined that it was showing, that my mum would come up and see it there on my mouth.

We'd never mentioned that kiss.

We'd been friends since childhood, Billy and I, much closer after his parents had got killed. He lived alone in his parents' house and we saw each other three or four times a week, sometimes more. We'd always been close but inexplicably, every now and then, I felt a compelling urge to touch him, or hug him or even, once or twice, to kiss him. I never did though; nothing had ever happened between us again.

Smiling at my thoughts, I took the mistletoe down from the mirror and dropped it into the bin. Then I went to bed.

The dead girl's picture was on the front page of the national newspaper the next morning. The headline was: POLICE MISS BODY IN SEARCH. Then, underneath: *Dead teenager not found for twenty-four hours; fifth victim. Questions raised in the House.*

The story went on but I couldn't take my eyes off the picture of the girl.

It was the same shot that they had shown on the telly the night before but it was larger and I sat and looked at it for minutes, while my mum chattered on about her students and their essays that were due in.

Then it dawned on me.

I knew the girl. I knew her face, had seen her recently.

I sat back and thought through my actions over the previous few days.

I stopped when I remembered following Mr Black. I was sitting in the playground, taking photos of him. Then I was sitting in the office looking through the photos. They had been all crooked and I had missed Mr Black out of two of them. I had caught the moody teenager. The one who had been sitting on the bench while Mr Black had played with his grandchild.

She had been sitting staring straight ahead and I had caught her in two of my photos.

The dead girl, Helen Driscoll, was the girl that I had seen in the park. The one that I had photo-graphed.

6
Ashes to Ashes

I went straight round to PHOTOKWIK.
On my way I kept picturing the girl's face, trying to re-create it in detail in my head. While I was waiting for the lights to change I closed my eyes for a few moments and saw her, legs stretched, lying back against the bench, her hands in her pockets, staring straight past me. She had a sullen expression, bored, as if she knew everything.

But I had thrown the photos away.

Two photos; both taken when Mr Black had bent down to pick up his grandchild. I had her there, on film, looking in the direction of the camera.

At 2.32. Thirty-two minutes past two.

The Railway Killer, Leslie Knight, had been captured at two-thirty.

I had Helen Driscoll still alive, on photo, at two thirty-two.

I dashed across the road and ran up the High Street before turning into PHOTOKWIK. The first person I saw was the kid who'd phoned me: Brian.

"We must stop meeting like this," he said, grinning.

"Is Larry in?" I said, ignoring him.

"Larry!" he shouted. "A certain young detective to see you."

I glared at him and he added, "Patsy Kelly here, wants a word."

Larry appeared through the swing doors and smiled when he saw me.

"Now then, what can I do for you? Some pictures, is it? Another rush job?"

"Larry," I puffed, "you know that film I gave you the other day, the one I wanted done quickly?"

"Certainly do? Is there something wrong with them? One or two a bit wonky?"

"No, it's just…"

Larry was often difficult to talk to. He was always asking questions and then answering them himself, before you got a chance to speak.

"I was wondering whether or not the developing machine…"

"The Kodak Deluxe," Larry said proudly.

"The Deluxe; whether it kept copies of what it developed?"

"You want copies of the negs? I can do copies for you."

"No, I wondered if the machine kept copies…"

I was losing my thread. Larry was looking at me with raised eyebrows. Brian was shuffling papers but I could tell that he was listening.

"Thing is, I lost the photos. My uncle will be furious. That's why I wondered if the machine kept copies."

"How did you lose them?" Larry said. "Fell out of your pocket? Oh, dear, no, the Deluxe doesn't keep a master-roll, Patsy. Are you sure you've lost them? They might be in your bedroom. My daughter's bedroom is a real state…"

I stood and let Larry babble on about the bedrooms of teenage girls and realized that the photos were gone.

The pictures I had of Helen Driscoll alive at the time that the serial killer was arrested were in the bottom of my uncle's office bin, under the tea bags and bits of sandwiches.

They were a pile of black ashes.

Billy took the common-sense approach.

"You don't know it was the same girl. You saw the face on the telly and *then* in the papers this morning. That's why it was familiar. Then you just thought back to the last teenager you'd seen. You've convinced yourself of something that isn't true."

I didn't answer him. I gulped down the tea he had made me and watched as he continued to iron. A small weekend bag was on the table, already half full.

"When are you going away?" I asked, changing the subject.

He looked at his watch.

"About five."

"It's very sudden, isn't it?" I said sulkily. Billy had made a last minute decision to visit his mum's sister who lived in Norfolk.

"That's true, but I've got no work on at the moment. She rang me before Christmas, asked me to come and I just put her off again. She lives on her own. The truth is," he said, "she's the only family I've got left. It seems silly not to keep in touch."

"Yes, I suppose so," I said, slightly miffed. I had got used to the fact that we were Billy's only family.

He was quiet for a moment and my mind wandered back to the teenager on the bench. When I concentrated I could see her whole face. It was as if my memory was like a camera and could zoom in to her features. She was sulky-looking, a kind of pout around her lips; she'd looked small, a young teenager. I pictured the school photograph; the smile had seemed forced, as if someone had insisted that she cheer up and she had obliged with the absolute minimum. Her hair had been shorter in the photograph as well. I was sure it was her. Certain.

"Why don't you come with me?" Billy said.

"Where?"

"To Norfolk. It's only for a few days. You'd like my aunt. We could do some sight-seeing. It'd be cold, but it could be fun."

Billy was right. It did sound like fun. I suddenly saw myself walking along a beach, the wind blowing my coat back, the spray of the sea in an arc behind me.

"I don't know," I said, feeling a tiny fist of excitement opening up in my chest. It wouldn't take me long to throw a few things in a suitcase. Two or three hats was all I would need.

"What about work?" I said vaguely, already tucking it away in the unimportant tray. The Helen Driscoll thing; I could write it all out and send it to Heather Warren; she could either look into it or dismiss it.

Then Billy said:

"Tony'll let you go! It's not as if you're doing anything important!"

He said it lightly, not meaning to hurt my feelings, but it hit me like a blow.

You're not doing anything important.

I looked at his cheerful face, his half-packed bag. I tried very hard to stop my feelings showing through but there must have been a crack in my composure because Billy, realizing what he'd said, put the iron down and came over.

"Oh, dear," he said. "I've said the wrong thing."

He squatted down on the floor beside my chair with his arm loosely around my shoulder.

"No," I said, self-pity welling up in my throat, "I suppose what I do isn't very important."

"Patsy," he said in a low voice, and his hand touched the skin at the back of my neck, "it was just a thoughtless thing to say. I didn't mean – "

"Yes, you did…" I turned round to him, my knees almost in his chest. "The day before yesterday I followed some poor old man around to catch him bending over. Yesterday, I harassed half a dozen people for money they owe my uncle; oh, and don't forget all the filing I did and the four cups of tea I made for Tony."

I stopped then and let the rest play on in my head. Billy rested his arms on my knees, drew a huge sigh and laid his head down. I felt his weight on my legs and didn't know what to do or say.

Nothing I did was very important. I was an office clerk who thought she was something better.

I lifted my hand nervously and put it on the back of Billy's head. A trip to Norfolk would be good for both of us. I let my fingers move in and out of his hair and found, after a few seconds, that I was holding my breath.

The iron hissed and broke the silence and Billy sat up.

"Well, Patricia, are you coming or not?" he said,

using my full name for once. For a fleeting moment I thought of Brian Martin and his clever chatter.

"Why not?" I said and stood up, my knees feeling strangely cold since Billy had leant off them. "I'll go and see Tony, then pack a few things in a bag. You could pick me up, about four-ish."

I don't know why I went back to the park where I had seen Helen Driscoll. I told myself it was just to confirm my story for Heather Warren, to find the exact bench, to copy the spelling of the precinct's name. It was on the way back to the office from Billy's house, give or take a few streets.

Whatever my reasons were, I ended up sitting on the bench that I had seen the girl sit on.

You're not doing anything important. Billy's words kept buzzing round my ears, threatening to sting me.

Why ever had I taken this job? Why hadn't I gone straight to university like my friends? A year off, I'd wanted. It had sounded good when I'd said it; as if I'd had some important project in my mind which I could do in the year. All summer long I'd felt excited. It had been a way of leaving college and still having that university place in my back pocket for the following year.

A job with my uncle's detective agency had sounded different. When I'd become involved with the Judy Hurst case I had felt important, even though I'd nearly been killed. Now, though, it was back to being Miss Office Clerk, Miss Teasmade, Miss Filing Clerk, Miss Fed-Up.

I sat for a few moments allowing myself to wallow in the injustice of my unimportant job and mundane life. Then I looked at my watch and shook myself. I got a small pad out of my bag and copied down the name of the precinct: Lister Square. I described the positioning of the bench by noting down the shop it was opposite: Majestic Dry Cleaners.

I put the pad away and just before I got up to leave I adopted the position that I remembered the girl was sitting in. I lazed back on the bench and let my legs lie casually apart. I put my hands in my pockets. I felt an inclination to let my head lean back against something but there was nothing behind me. The girl must have held up her head rigidly for it to sit like that. It was odd. For the rest of her to look so relaxed and yet for her head to be so tense. Had it been Helen Driscoll? Was I absolutely sure?

I let my hands fall out of my pocket and found my fingers playing with an indent in the wood. I glanced down and saw some lettering.

I sat forward and zipped up my jacket. The Asian lady was out in her sari again although this time she had a padded coat over the top. She shouted at a small child who was walking along past the car shop. I wondered if Mr Black had been here since that day with his grandchild.

I found myself staring down again at the lettering that someone had dug into the bench. There were several sets of initials and then, further along, in an area which no one had used, was a new set: HD 101.

I sat very still looking at it. It didn't mean anything, I kept telling myself. HD. Lots of people had those initials. Even if it was Helen Driscoll, she could have gone there at any time and carved her initials. 101. One hundred and one, 101, the tenth of the first. The tenth of January.

And then I remembered. When Mr Black had struggled up with his grandchild, the teenager had been digging away at the bench, ignoring what was happening.

It had been Helen Driscoll, carving her initials in the bench.

I was sure now and nobody, not even Billy, was going to change my mind.

7
A Career in the Police

I went straight back to the office and made a phone call.

"Patsy," Heather Warren said, after I'd finally been connected to her extension, "sorry about the difficulties in getting through. You don't know how awful the press have been over these Railway Murders. How are you?"

"Fine," I said, my voice trembling slightly. "Have I rung at a really difficult time?"

"It's always a difficult time! How's old Tony these days, although don't tell him I said he was 'old'. You know how touchy these menopausal men can be!"

My uncle had worked with Heather when he'd been in CID. She wasn't one of his favourite people.

"I was wondering," I said, getting straight to the point, "whether I could take you up on your offer about having a look around the station. I'm finding my role here a bit limited; only don't tell Tony I said that."

"Of course not," she said and I could hear the pleasure in her voice. "You thinking of joining up then? About time you made a positive career move."

"I'm thinking about it," I said.

"You could spend a day with me, maybe week after next – "

"I was really wondering," I butted in, "if I could come this week, maybe tomorrow. I wouldn't have to stay with you, I know how busy you are, I could just shadow some junior officer. It might even be a more realistic experience for me." I was speaking rapidly, hoping she wouldn't butt in and put me off. She started to say something a couple of times, but then became more quiet as I went on.

"Good idea, Patsy. You're right, of course; a day with me wouldn't be at all representational of what a young officer could expect. It would be much more sensible for you to go with one of my juniors. Let me fix it up for – "

"Tomorrow?" I said. "Tony's out all day in court so he wouldn't know about it. I don't want to hurt his feelings."

"Tomorrow?" She sounded unsure. I could hear the sound of paper being ruffled, as though she was looking something up. "At a push I could probably manage tomorrow. About ten; see you then." The line went dead and I felt a moment of exhilaration.

A day in the station would give me access to details about the Railway Murders. I was hoping that in my totally innocent way I could ask some questions about the case: the *exact* time that Leslie Knight was picked up, the *precise* time of Helen's death.

I sat back, my heart thumping with tension. I looked at my watch.

It was going on for three o'clock. Billy would be at my house in about an hour to take me off to Norfolk. I needed to get home to explain to him why I couldn't go. Doing it on the phone would be no good at all.

There was no one in when I got home. I put on the central heating as well as the kitchen light. Even that early it seemed to be greying over, the sky looking heavier, the clouds dense and solid.

I took off my glasses to clean them and thought about what I would say to Billy. I knew I wasn't going to tell him that I was staying behind for Helen Driscoll. He might think it was because of what he had said to me, that I wasn't doing anything *important*.

The doorbell rang and I went to answer it.

"Your car awaits," Billy said when I opened the door.

"I can't go," I said, taking him by the sleeve and pulling him into the hallway.

"Why not?" he said, looking concerned for a moment. He changed his expression when I didn't answer. "Is it because of this girl at the precinct?"

"No, no," I lied.

Just then the phone rang and he took a step backwards towards the front door. I left it ringing and followed him, grabbing his arm.

"Tony needs me in the office. He's in court all day tomorrow and a new client's coming in. He's going to let me do the initial interview. It will be good experience for me." I was making it up as I went along.

Billy looked straight at me, then he softened.

The phone had stopped ringing and the answerphone had come on.

We're not available to come to the phone at the moment, my mum's teacher's voice sounded in the hall.

"It's good experience for me, Billy. I'll never get anywhere in this job if I don't throw myself into it." I was beginning to believe it myself.

Please leave a message and we'll get back to you, my mum's voice continued.

Billy was smiling. "All right, Pat, a girl's got to do what a girl's got to do!" He leant over and gave me a peck on the cheek. I closed my eyes for the mini-second that it took and was just about to speak when

I heard a familiar voice leaving a message on the answer-phone.

"Listen, Miss Patsy Kelly, I know you really want to go out with me and that you're just playing hard to get. Why don't we take in a film tonight…"

The smile fell off Billy's face and for a brief moment he flinched as if he'd been hit by something.

Embarrassed and flustered I turned and took three giant steps down the hallway to pick up the phone.

"Brian, will you get off this phone and stop harassing me," I said.

"I love it when you're angry," was his reply.

I slammed down the phone and turned around, my mouth open ready to explain. Billy had gone though and the front door was swinging open in the darkening afternoon. I ran out, down the pathway, only to see his car disappearing up the street.

I went back into my hallway and glared at the phone, not sure what had just happened, exactly why Billy had gone off in such an abrupt way.

At least that's what I told myself.

8
CID

The next morning I went into the office and noted down a couple of messages from the answer-phone. I ruffled the files around and left an open one on my desk. I left one of my drawers hanging open and put a note on top of my work: *Just popped out for a while – Patsy.*

I was banking on the fact that Tony would be in court all day. If for some reason he came into the office he would see the note and assume that I'd be back shortly.

Before leaving I looked at the phone with some agitation, wondering whether or not to ring Billy at his aunt's. I decided against it.

If Billy or my uncle had seen me that morning they

would have been much surprised. I had adopted my young career girl disguise. Even my mum's face had dropped when she'd seen me slipping out of the front door.

I'd put my mum's heated rollers all over my head and my hair had bounced out and made a soft halo of curls around my face. I'd got out my make-up bag and sat for a while deciding which face to put on.

A lot of time I don't bother with make-up. I have no objections to it in principle but it can be time-consuming and it means you have to be careful all day not to scratch your nose or rub your eyelids. It also means, once you've applied it, that you have to check from time to time that it is all still there, in place, otherwise you look a bit daft, especially if you have only one bright blue eyelid or one cheek rouged and the other not.

When I did wear it though, I liked to decide on a look.

Getting ready to go to the police station I had decided to go for pastel colours, nothing too threatening. I'd put some light blue on my eyelids and some grey mascara. I'd put on some pale beige foundation and used a spot stick to cover up one or two red areas. I didn't use blusher and I'd put on some very pale pink lipstick.

I'd put on my glasses to see what it looked like.

I'd looked in my mum's wardrobe and found a close-fitting dress that she hadn't worn for a while.

It was shorter than the things I wore but I'd put on some opaque tights so that my legs didn't feel so exposed. I'd put a suit jacket on top of it and found a small scarf in one of my drawers that I made into a sort of cravat.

I'd found some tiny pearl earrings and sprayed some of my mum's scent around my neck.

I'd decided against a hat. It was a mark of eccentricity and I didn't want to appear odd at the station. I'd put some things into a small handbag and taken a look at myself in the mirror.

I'd looked like someone's secretary. The dress, somewhat tighter on me than on my mum, restricted my stride and meant that I had to take shorter steps. I'd smiled at myself. I definitely looked sweet, nice, easy-going: Miss Perfect WPC.

My mum, who'd been talking on the phone, had looked at me in amazement as I'd come down the stairs.

"It's all right," I'd said in a loud whisper, "I'm working deep undercover."

I was taken straight to the CID suite. Heather Warren was in a meeting when I arrived but a young man in jeans and a suit jacket got me a mug of tea. He gave it to me abruptly and some of it sloshed over the side and on to the desk and my leg.

"I'm Des," he said. "You'll be shadowing me today."

I smiled but he didn't. I put the tea on the desk and got out some tissues to wipe up the mess. Des hadn't noticed and was intent on looking through some papers. A woman cleaner appeared at my shoulder.

"Here, dear," she said, mopping up the mess with a J-cloth. She picked up my sopping tissues and dropped them into a large black plastic bag that she had. Then she continued on up the room, emptying ashtrays and wiping surfaces.

The "suite" was a long area with three glassed-off rooms along the side. One side of it was lined with windows and there was still spray snow stuck along them and the remains of a "Merry Christmas". There were about ten desks and a number of filing cabinets. A number of Christmas cards were still stuck to the filing cabinets and I could see a half-full bottle of red wine standing, corkless, on top of one of them. Along the back wall was a line of computer terminals, each of them with someone sitting in front. The walls were covered with several maps and there was a large white board in the corner that had writing all over it.

"Working as a *private detective*, Miss Kelly," Des said, smiling and nodding at his papers.

"Patsy, please," I said, less friendly this time. Des wasn't ecstatic about having me with him.

Just then I heard a voice.

"Patsy!" It was Heather Warren. She came

striding across the room, numerous people moving out of her way, one or two hastily stubbing cigarettes out on to ashtrays. "You're looking well, Patsy!" she said, an unlit cigarette between her fingers. "Des and Stevie will look after you today. I'm very busy this morning but I'll probably see you later this afternoon."

She didn't wait for me to answer but turned away and in a loud voice said: "People!"

The sounds in the office lessened.

"Plan for today as follows: meeting in ten minutes in the conference room for update on the Leslie Knight case; apart from that, there's the burglaries on the Selby Estate, Tricia – you, Terry and Leon follow that up; the fake welfare workers have been active again over in Archer Street; Peter – you and Mac follow that up…"

Heather went on but I was thinking about the meeting in ten minutes in the conference room on the Leslie Knight case. I was hoping – praying – that Des Murray was part of that team.

He wasn't.

"Des – you and Stevie, and Patsy, of course," she smiled, "go down to the Harley youth centre and see if you can find out any more about who's bringing drugs into the place."

Then she walked back up the room and disappeared into an office.

A couple of people let out sighs, as though they'd

been holding their breaths all the while she'd been speaking.

"Are you coming then?" Des Murray was rattling his car keys. I looked round the office with frustration. Some people were tucking important-looking files under their arms and getting ready for the meeting in the conference room. I was on my way to a youth centre to find out about drugs.

It hadn't been part of my plan.

Outside, it was a bright winter's day, the sun glittering against a blue sky, bouncing off windows and dazzling us when we looked around. The wind whizzed around though, lifting the ends of my coat and pulling my hair all to one side. It had an icy edge and I felt goose-pimples rise on my arms.

In the car I made the best of it. I didn't have much choice. Des silently chain-smoked and Stevie, a woman of about thirty, ate constantly: cough sweets, chocolate bars, cakes, chewing gum. She also chatted to me the whole way. She'd known my uncle – well, briefly – at least she'd seen him around. She'd wanted to do A-levels but the teachers didn't like her; at least, one male teacher picked on her all the time. She'd considered going private; at least a friend of hers knew someone who worked Security in a big department store. They paid good money but there wasn't the job security. She had boyfriends, not many of them serious because they couldn't take her job; at least they didn't like the fact that she had to work closely with so many men.

We both looked at Des Murray when she said this; he had just inhaled a lungful of cigarette smoke and was looking peaceful and sublime. His hands were on the steering wheel and I noticed a heavy gold ring on his finger. It glinted confidently in the sunlight.

We went to the youth centre but it was all locked up. A note pinned to the door said that the youth worker was off sick.

"What shall we do?" Stevie said. "Go round his house?"

"No," Des said, "let's take a walk through the flats."

As we walked through the flats the wind sliced past us, blasting at us head-on round the corners. We were heading for a small sweetshop that had bars over the windows and an entryphone at the door. On the brick wall underneath someone had sprayed "Fort Knox" in untidy lettering.

Des went up to the door. "I need some fags," he said and after speaking into the wall he was allowed in.

Stevie said: "Don't mind Des, he's just annoyed at being taken off the Railway Murders."

"For me?" I said perplexed.

"No. Now that they've got Leslie Knight, it's

being trimmed down. Half a dozen detectives were reassigned yesterday. Des was one of them."

The door of the shop opened and Des came out with the flicker of a smile on his face.

"Let's go and see old Florrie Roberts," he said.

"Florrie?" Stevie said. "Florrie's at it again? After what the magistrate said?"

"She probably believes that her great age will protect her from prison. Maybe not this time."

"An old-age pensioner is dealing drugs?" I said incredulously.

"Maybe," Des said, lighting a cigarette. "Some grannies just knit jumpers for their grandchildren; Florrie looks after a few pills."

As we went up the stairs Stevie nudged me. "Keep away from the old girl," she said, "she's got a nasty pinch."

I sat in the front seat with Des; Florrie and Stevie sat in the back. On the floor at my feet were several small bags of tablets. Florrie's white hair was permed into tight curls. She had drop-pearl earrings on and a red T-shirt that said "Majorca" across the front.

Des had found the drugs in an ornamental tea pot.

"She leaves them there every time. No imagin-ation," he said.

"I'm saying *nothing*," was all Florrie had said.

It took until after lunch time to process Florrie, and I was allowed to have a walk around on my own. I had a visitor's badge on and I had a quick look at the interview rooms, the cells, the communications area, the offices, the canteen, everywhere.

After a while I came on the conference room which had a "NO ENTRY" sign on the door. I took a quick look around to make sure no one saw me and went in. The room was empty and I closed the door quietly behind me.

The far wall was covered with photos, maps and writing. The words "OPERATION ROSE" were written in block letters at the top of a white board. I walked closer and saw, with shock, that the photos were all of the dead bodies of the murdered girls. My eye jumped from one to another, not really looking at faces, but at the dark marks on the necks of the girls, the open mouths, the tip of the tongues. They were unrecognizable from their school photographs.

I looked away to quell a sensation of nausea.

There was an overhead projector and several files piled on the table. There was a computer monitor with words typed on half the screen. It probably meant that someone had been working in there and would be back any minute. I had to be quick. My hand shaking, I took my notepad out of my handbag and, holding my breath, I looked through the files;

just underneath "KATE HARGREAVES" was "HELEN DRISCOLL".

I looked round again, my heart noticeably thumping, and opened the file.

I didn't read what was there, I just copied everything I saw. I would read it later. My hand scribbled down every detail that I could see. The first page done, I turned over and jotted down stuff from another sheet. I looked up at the white board. At the top corner, written in giant blue lettering, were the words: "LESLIE KNIGHT CAUGHT 2.30, 10TH JAN!!!" They were ringed with red and stood out delightedly. Around them were odd phrases and words that I jotted down. A voice from outside the door made me stop and put my notepad away. It was time to go. I took a last look around and for the first time my eye was caught by small photographs of roses pinned down the edge of the board. I glanced at them for a second, then turned and walked quickly out of the room.

As I closed the door and walked away a WPC passed me with a mug of steaming coffee. She went into the conference room and I stopped and leant against the wall to catch my breath. I felt as if I'd just done a half-hour run.

Des Murray was still in the midst of paperwork. Stevie was in the toilets. I joined her there in front of a mirror. She was painting a dark line across each eyelid. I got some bits of my own make-up out and tried to look as if I was concerned about my face. I tutted loudly and got out my eye-shadow.

"This stuff's always coming off," I said.

"I know," she answered.

"What's 'Operation Rose'?" I asked, squirting a dollop of foundation on to my finger and dotting it over my cheeks.

"That's the code name for the Leslie Knight case. It's a bit confidential really, but now that he's caught I don't suppose it matters."

"Oh, the one Des got taken off," I said, as though that was the only interest the case could have for me. "He's really fed up about it, isn't he?"

"I should say. He's been a real pain ever since. I can understand it really. You work with a case, go through all the hard bits, looking at the bodies, telling the mums and dads, house-to-house enquiries and then, when they get someone or it starts going right, when there might be some *satisfaction* in it, you get pulled off. It's not fair."

"The rose then; that's just a name, something someone thought up?"

"No, no, it's to do with the roses that we found on the bodies."

"Roses?" I said, my pink lipstick in mid-air.

"Yes, well, it's confidential too, but it'll come out in a couple of days, I'm sure. The police always try to keep some detail back from the press. It's to stop people confessing to the crime. You wouldn't believe how many people want to confess to a murder!"

"What did they keep back?" I said, a grumbling sense of unease growing inside me. I scooped up my make-up and shoved it back into my bag.

"On each of the bodies there was a rose. He strangled them with rope, then left a rose, a single rose, lying on their chests."

"On all of them? Even Helen Driscoll?" I said, feeling my case crumble before my eyes.

"On each of them. How perverted can you get? He kills them, then leaves a rose. Weird bloke." Stevie was patting her lips with a tissue.

A rose was left on Helen Driscoll's chest. It must mean that she had been killed by Leslie Knight; just like the other girls.

9
A Rose by Any Other Colour

I let Stevie's words sink in while I ate my lunch.
We were in an unmarked car at the end of the
High Road, parked opposite a cash-dispensing
machine. We were on the look-out for a group of
muggers who worked round the area.

All the time, in my head, there was an argument
going on. Helen Driscoll was killed by the same
man who had killed the other girls. He had left a
rose on their bodies and he left a rose on hers. But
Leslie Knight was caught by the police at 2.30 p.m.
I had seen Helen Driscoll *alive* at 2.32 p.m.

Des was smoking in the passenger seat and Stevie
was talking about police work being a good job,
provided you didn't expect to have a private life.
She kept giving examples and then saying: *isn't that*

right, Des?, to which he answered a few words. He even had a stab at a joke. Once or twice he commented on women who passed by the car.

I decided to try and take advantage of Des's lighter mood. I kept my voice casual, as if I were just chatting, passing the time of day.

"You were involved in the Railway Killer investigation, weren't you, Des?"

"Um…" he answered.

"My mum's friend is obsessed with that case," I said. "I'd love to be able to tell her a few things about it."

"Confidential," Des said, not wasting any words.

"Oh, go on, Des. Everything will be out in a few days anyway," Stevie said, giving Des a push on the arm.

Des looked around reluctantly, only the suggestion of a smile on his lips.

"It'll be good for the kid to go home and tell her mum's mate a few unknown details," Stevie said. I bristled inwardly at being called a kid but said nothing.

"You tell her then."

"No, you," Stevie said, nudging him.

They were like a pair of silly boys in school. I almost expected Stevie to give Des a half nelson…

"What do you want to know?" Des said in a bored voice, but I noticed that, for once, there wasn't a cigarette in his mouth.

"Well," I said, "why did he do it? How did he do it?"

"Oh, you don't want to know much then," Des said, throwing a smile sideways at Stevie.

"He was a ticket collector, wasn't he?" I asked, deliberately getting it wrong, hoping to get Des started.

"No, no; Leslie Knight was a ticket *inspector* for British Rail. He worked on the Liverpool Street line. Three of the victims used the train to go to school, posh schools, up in the city. Another used the train recently to go up to a London museum, and the last one, the Driscoll girl, had a friend in Bethnal Green whom she'd visited at least twice recently." He spoke in a sing-song voice, as though he'd learnt it all off by heart. "We think that Knight asked to see their passes or some other form of identification, a travel card or whatever. He probably took a note of their names and addresses and then approached the girls when they were out somewhere, tricking them into his van.

"There are traces of fibre from the clothes of three of the girls in the back of his van. The second and the fifth one haven't yet made a match."

I was trying to look impressed; inside my head there was frantic activity going on, repeating and memorizing the things he was saying, trying to listen hard to make sure I didn't miss anything.

"So there were no fibres for the Driscoll girl," I said.

"No."

"Weird bloke," I said, as though that was my only interest in the story, as though it was a bit of gossip for me. "Fancy leaving roses."

Des looked at Stevie.

"I was just chatting to her. It'll be all over the papers soon," she said shrugging her shoulders.

"You've told her everything already!"

"Roses," I kept on. "I wonder what colour they were?"

"Yellow and red," Des said.

"Yellow and red?"

"Yeah, he was changing his colour just as we caught him. He left a yellow one on the Driscoll girl's body."

A yellow rose. A *yellow rose* was left on Helen, not a red one.

Just then Des opened the car door and got out and slammed it. He walked a few metres and went into a paper shop. I said:

"Imagine what the press would make of the roses."

"It'll be in all the papers tomorrow, probably. Now that the case is sewn up. It won't be the only thing the press has got to talk about," she said. "Soon they'll know about John Martin's son and the Driscoll girl."

"John Martin?"

"He's a uniformed inspector. Been around for donkey's years. His son apparently went to the same school as the Driscoll girl and he went out with her for a few months. It finished a while ago. Don't tell Des I told you that."

I said nothing as Des got back into the car.

I felt weighted down with all the information I'd been given in the previous few minutes.

"Here," Des said and threw a bar of chocolate into the back seat and one at Stevie.

"Thanks," I said and we sat in silence for a few minutes. Then Des said:

"There's nothing happening here, Stevie. Let's go back to base."

We got back to the station at about two o'clock. I went straight into the loos and jotted down everything that Des and Stevie had said – as much of it as I could remember. Just as I came out of the cubicle, Heather Warren walked into the toilets.

"Patsy!" she said. "How's your day been?"

"Great," I said. "Des and Stevie have been really nice."

"Good. Stevie's a good policewoman," Heather said. I noticed she said nothing about Des.

"Yes," I said, closing my bag. I was keen to go back to the office. I wanted to be alone so that I could sort out all the things I had heard.

"Tell you what," she said, "why don't you finish off your day with me? I've just got one more visit to make and then I'll drop you back to Tony's office. It should only take about an hour."

"I don't know," I said, looking at my watch. I needed to be alone. To think it all through.

"It could be interesting, if a bit morbid. I need to go and close the scene of crime where the last murdered girl was found, Helen Driscoll. It might be good for you to see what it's like."

I almost swallowed my tongue with surprise.

"I'll get my coat," I said.

We drove to the scene of crime in the back of a dark unmarked car. As we got closer I felt my tension level rising; it was as though she was taking me to see Helen Driscoll's actual body, rather than just the place she'd been found. As we reached the gate of the old yard I saw flowers stacked up along the pavement. Dozens of tiny bouquets left presumably by members of the public. Beside them was a sign: *KEEP OUT, POLICE INVESTIGATION.* Someone had even draped a child's teddy bear over that. As we went into the yard there were metres of white ribbon strung up between the buildings, and a single policeman was standing outside a door that was closed.

The yard was criss-crossed with railway tracks, mostly sunk into the concrete, so we just drove across. When we parked I got out of the car and looked around.

It was an area about the size of a football pitch,

mostly open with a couple of buildings along the side. There were some small wooden sheds over by the entrance and a van that had its wheels removed. There was something painted on the side of the van, a name, stylized, in chunky lettering: JACKO.

"This way, Patsy," Heather said, striding ahead. She stopped for a few seconds and talked to the policeman who was standing guard.

Then we walked through the door into the dark interior of the warehouse. There was no lighting, although a portable lamp on a stand had been erected. Heather turned it on and it suddenly looked as though we were inside a small theatre. As if some actors were going to come on and start a play.

On the ground, half on top of some sacking, was the outline of Helen Driscoll's body. It was a strong white line drawn carefully, the way that kids do sometimes when they're drawing outlines of their hand.

"Oh," was all I said.

I'd seen a dead body once before. It had been pale and doll-like. The girl had been lying still, her eyes open; like a model for an artist. My breath had caught in my throat and my limbs had gone weak and jelly-like.

There was no body this time but I still felt uneasy. The dark corners of the warehouse seemed sinister and the bright light harsh and unreal. For a brief moment I got flashes in my head; pictures that I'd seen of the dead girls lying flat on their backs, no breath left inside them, their mouths open as if in a silent cry.

"She was a tiny girl, you know," Heather said. "She was only five foot one. I'm sure she couldn't have put up much of a fight. We found her almost twenty-four hours after we caught him."

"Really," I said, dragging my eyes away from the white-line drawing on the floor.

"He must have killed her and then walked out of here and on to the road. His van was parked there, about a hundred metres down. For some reason he didn't go away. That's one thing I don't understand. Why didn't he just go home? He'd done it the other times. No, he wandered off towards the Regent's Road depot."

"That was where he was caught."

"Only minutes later! That's what's so frustrating. He never said a word. Just sat silently in the back of the police car when metres away, two minutes' walk away, was the dead girl."

Heather picked up a torch and shone it into the far corners of the warehouse. The beam of light caught two eyes looking at us. Then they disappeared.

"Rats," Heather said.

"Oh."

"She lay here for twenty-four hours before anyone found her."

I felt as though I was going to shiver and tensed myself. Twenty-four hours in that dark, cold, rat-infested place.

"When was she killed? I mean, what time exactly. You caught him at two-thirty, I think."

"Yes, we did. We chased him up the railway tracks. We were lucky that a train wasn't coming the other way."

Heather clicked off the light switch and the warehouse was black again.

Walking out she said, "Forensics say that she'd been lying there from twenty-four to twenty-six hours."

"Can't they be exact?" I said, trying to sound interested in the science of forensics.

"Not really. They can sometimes, but in this case the overnight temperature was below freezing so it's not possible to give a precise time. They think it was probably between, say, one o'clock and two-thirty."

We walked out into the daylight and I found myself inhaling as much air as I could.

"I've just got a couple of things to arrange with the constable, Patsy, then we'll go." Heather walked across to the PC and within seconds he was smiling at something she said.

I walked through the yard to the gate and looked at the border of cut flowers that sat on the pavement; reds and yellows, blues and whites. Some were dying, had been there for days but some were new, perhaps only laid there that morning.

It was a touching sight. People who had never known Helen Driscoll feeling grief at the manner of her death. The flowers placed closely together looked like a giant garland. It was almost festive; there was nothing funereal about it.

I bent down to look at a new bunch that had been placed on top of some dying blooms. There may have been more than thirty assorted flowers inside the cellophane. Also inside it was a small card.

I glanced at some of the other bouquets. They too had cards. People had written messages on them like: *with sympathy; so young; to sweet Helen; we won't forget you.*

The small card inside the new bouquet had a more personal message on it though: *Helen, you should have got to know me better*. I wasn't sure what it meant. I could see Heather, in the car, coming towards me, so I said it over and over in my head.

When I got into the car Heather said:

"Do you think it's been worth it; today, I mean? Have you learned something?"

"Yes," I said, my notebook and my head full of details. "I've learned more than I thought I would."

10
Decisions

Heather dropped me back at the office. As soon as I got in the door I wrote down the message from the bouquet of flowers: *Helen, you should have got to know me better*. I didn't want to forget the wording.

There was no sign that Tony had been there. I put the kettle on and looked at my notebook. It was full of scribbled sentences, words that I'd underlined or circled. I read all of it over three or four times and then sat back to think.

There were a number of possibilities, the main one being that the girl I had seen was not Helen Driscoll. All sorts of things pointed in that direction. Helen Driscoll had been killed in the same way as the other victims of Leslie Knight, strangled with a piece of climbing rope. There was a rose left on her body, just the same as the others. She was fifteen (even if she hadn't looked it) and was still at school, exactly the same as the others.

But I was sure I had seen her *alive* at the time that Leslie Knight was picked up. If I were right it must mean that someone else murdered her and tried to make it look like she was another victim of the serial killer.

I looked at my notes that I'd copied from her file. She had lived with her mother and father, Elizabeth and Peter Driscoll. She had one brother, Joe, who was about a year younger. Her family were quite well off and she went to the local secondary school. She was an ordinary girl, not unlike the other victims.

There were some important differences though. The other girls were all "high-fliers". Helen Driscoll was not; in fact it said in the notes that she *"had been a problem in school and had recently taken to truanting regularly"*. The other girls, Des had said, had all been using the railway for school or educational matters. That might have meant that they were in school uniform. Helen Driscoll, though, had used the train to see a friend who lived in Bethnal Green, so presumably she had been wearing her own clothes, not uniform.

The dead girls all had red roses left on their bodies. Helen Driscoll's rose was yellow.

The alleged killer, Leslie Knight, killed Helen Driscoll, but instead of then going home, he'd stalked another railway yard to make another killing. This was completely out of step with the previous murders where he had made just one killing.

There were none of Helen Driscoll's clothes fibres in Leslie Knight's van (although they hadn't found any of Kate Hargreaves' fibres either).

The kettle had boiled and clicked itself off. I sat and looked at it and began to think of a possible explanation.

What if someone had the motive and desire to kill Helen Driscoll. The newspapers were full of the gory details about the serial killer and the Railway Murders. Why not make the murder look like that? Then she would have been just one of the victims of a killer who would perhaps never be caught and even if he was, wouldn't be believed.

But no member of the public knew about the roses.

So, whoever it was had to have some link to someone who worked in the police station, someone with access to confidential information.

I remembered Stevie's words: *soon they'll be talking about Inspector Martin's son and the Driscoll girl.*

Helen Driscoll had gone out with a boy for a few months whose father was a police inspector. What was I thinking? That the boy and his father plotted to murder Helen Driscoll and covered it up by making it look like one of the serial killer's murders?

Why would they do it?

My suspicions were getting out of hand. It was ridiculous. I needed to talk to Billy so that he could calm me down, straighten the whole thing out.

I sat back in my chair and looked at the phone, wondering whether or not to ring him. I got out my diary and looked up the Norfolk number in the back. Something stopped me though. I got up and made a cup of tea instead.

The trouble with Billy was that he was just too sensible, he would never take chances. I'd known him since secondary school and he was the kind of kid who wore the complete uniform day after day. All his exercise books were covered and his homework done.

He wasn't a boffin or a goody-goody, it was just that he liked to do things properly. He was good at knowing our rights as pupils and anyone who had had the rough edge of some teacher's tongue went and shared it with Billy. When I first knew him he was always talking about suing people. If a computer game went wrong or a bus conductor shoved us off the bus he would shout: *I'll sue you; I could sue him, you know!*

He calmed down over the years but he was always

arguing with the teachers, or disputing some adult rule.

Billy was an only child and so was I. It was the thing we had in common, no siblings. We sort of drifted together, long-time friends. He was the person I always went to if I was upset or annoyed with anyone. He was good at talking me out of things; a proposed fight with a big girl in the year above who'd said I'd been talking about her behind her back; a plan to play a practical joke on a new teacher; a scheme to write the irregular French verbs all down my right leg so that I wouldn't get poor marks in a test.

Don't do it, Patsy, he'd say, and most of the time, I took his advice.

Sometimes I didn't though, like the time my friends Sherry and Beth and I told our parents that we were staying at each other's houses for the night, when in fact we stayed out all night, at a club until about three o'clock, then an all-night café, then a walk through Hyde Park at dawn.

The sheer daring and naughtiness of it had thrilled me and even though we'd ended up dog-tired with wrinkled clothes I'd not regretted it. It had been an *adventure*. There had been an element of *danger* involved.

That was something Billy could never under-stand. When I'd told him about it afterwards his forehead had wrinkled and he'd shaken his head like a wise old man who simply didn't understand the younger generation.

We'd always known that Billy had been born with the common-sense of a thirty-year-old. He just didn't take chances.

And I did. That was the difference between us.

I dialled the Norfolk number and let it ring a few times, then just as I heard the phone being answered I put the receiver back down, cutting the line dead.

If I spoke to Billy about Helen Driscoll he would put me off taking the case any further. I needed to make a decision about whether to pursue the investigation, as I had done with the Judy Hurst murder, and I had to make that decision on my own.

It wasn't even as simple as that. Even if I wanted to follow up the case I couldn't think of a way to move forward without being able to talk to the girl's family, her friends, her boyfriend, Inspector Martin's son. How could I? I wasn't a police officer and I wasn't officially investigating the case.

Why should anybody talk to me?

I heard footsteps on the stairs outside and saw my uncle come into the office.

"Hi," I said lightly, closing my notebook and pushing it into my bag.

"My God, Patricia, what've you done to your-self? You look lovely," Tony said.

I'd forgotten about my career girl disguise, my bouncy hair and short dress.

"I wish you'd dress like that more often," he said, taking his overcoat off and hanging it up on the hook.

"Um..." I said. He went into his office and closed the door. A second or so later the intercom came on:

"Patricia, can you get me the Missing Persons' file and a nice cup of tea."

I let the water reheat and thought back to the day I'd seen Helen Driscoll lounging on the bench in the park, looking steadfastly at something in front of her, digging out her initials on the bench that she was sitting on. I closed my eyes for a minute and tried to visualize her. I could see her shape and the colour of her hair and for a mini-second I focused on her face. It was Helen Driscoll, I was sure; as sure as I could be.

The picture in my head began to fade though and all at once it was gone. I tried hard for a few moments to reconstruct it but it was blurred and featureless.

I was losing the memory of that scene. Soon I wouldn't be able to visualize her at all.

I got the Missing Persons' file and took it and the tea through to my uncle.

"Thanks," he said. He'd taken off his suit jacket and was sitting with his shirt-sleeves rolled up. He looked as if he was too hot.

"I bumped into an admirer of yours today," he said.

"Really?" I said. "Who?"

"Young Brian, from the developers."

"You mean PHOTOKWIK."

"He seems smitten by you."

"Don't be silly," I said, pulling the hem of my mum's skirt down. My uncle was always using old-fashioned words like "smitten". He once asked me if Billy and I were "courting".

"You could do worse," he said, "he's a nice young lad. He's got a good job. His family are…"

"Tony, I'm not interested in him, or his family. He's not my type," I said, my cheeks heating up. The last thing I needed was Tony trying to fix me up with a boyfriend from a nice family.

"His dad's a police inspector. I thought you were considering police work."

"Really?" I said, trying to sound interested.

"Nice man. He and I collaborated on a number of cases," Tony said. "I can remember a house-breaking case that we worked on for weeks…"

And then it came to me.

Brian at PHOTOKWIK's dad was a police inspector. Further back, somewhere on the edges of my memory, were his words the first time I met him: *Brian Martin, at your service.*

"They used to shift their stuff at car-boot sales," Tony was reminiscing.

Inspector Martin was Brian's dad. He was Brian Martin's dad!

I waited, bursting with agitation, while my uncle continued his story.

"We posed as punters, he and I, browsing round the boot sales."

"Actually, Tony," I said, breaking into his story, "I said I'd give Mum a ring a while ago, so I ought to get on with it."

"Sure," he said, waving me out with his hand. Closing the door I could hear him talking quietly to himself: *Car-boot sales, whatever next...*

Brian Martin was too old to have been Helen Driscoll's boyfriend. There was one other explanation. I dialled the number of PHOTOKWIK. He answered straight away.

"Hi, Brian," I said, "it's Patsy Kelly."

"Pat," he said, immediately irking me by shortening my name. I kept my composure and continued:

"Brian, I'm really sorry I was a bit short the other day; your phone call came at a bad time for me."

"That's all right – " he started to speak.

"Hey, my uncle Tony was telling me about your dad working with him when he was a policeman. What a small world!" I rushed on, not giving him a chance to speak. "It's terrible about the Railway Murders though. I'll bet your brother's upset, you know, about his ex being one of the victims." I had my fingers crossed; I was willing him to answer the way I wanted him to.

"A bit, I suppose," he said, "but it's been over between them for a while."

"Awful business." I was almost jumping up and down in my chair. "Listen Brian, I wanted to take you up on that offer you made, for a meal or a drink. What about tonight?"

"Yes, OK. Where?"

"Why don't I meet you at that pizza place over the road from the shop. Say about seven. We can have a chat."

"OK, see you then."

I put the phone down and looked around. My uncle was standing at the door of his office smirking at me.

"In my day, it was the men who asked the women out. Call me old-fashioned but I liked it that way."

11
Dating

I sat in the pizza parlour and had a drink while I waited for Brian Martin to arrive. I had some very mild misgivings about being there on the basis of a date.

I had no choice though. He was the only link I had with Helen Driscoll.

I'd also discarded my pretty girl disguise. I'd nestled into my jeans and put a giant silk shirt on top. I'd unpeeled the tights and found a warm pair of wool socks and my DMs. I had my heavy overcoat on and a tight, floppy-brimmed velvet hat that my mum had found in a car-boot sale.

I'd given my face a good wash too and put a couple of thick black lines on my eyes and some maroon lipstick. I looked a bit Gothic. It suited my purposes. I didn't want to appear too inviting for Brian Martin.

He came just after seven. I waved to him as he walked in the door.

"Hi," he said. "I'm not late, am I?"

"No," I said. "Have a seat."

"You look a million dollars," he said, and I cringed.

"Thanks," I said, making a mental note to avoid the Gothic look in all future visits to PHOTO-KWIK.

He sat opposite me and for a minute neither of us said anything.

I suddenly felt very awkward and embarrassed to be there. He picked up the menu and started to read it intently.

"Let me see..." he said, as though he was con-sidering his choices. "I'll have Italian sausage pizza, garlic bread, a salad and a drink."

"Same for me," I said, giving him a jolly smile.

I wasn't prepared for what happened next. He reached across the table and took one of my hands into his and held it tightly.

"I was really pleased when you rang me, Pat. I really like you."

"Oh," I said, feeling my hand squeezed hard.

The waitress came and he let my hand go. I pulled it back across the table and kept it safe in my lap. We ordered our meal and then Brian leaned across the table and said, in a low voice, "I love the hat."

"Thanks. I was in the police station today, where your dad works." I decided to plunge straight in. I didn't know how long I was going to be able to put up with his interest in me. It might be that I shortly got an attack of food-poisoning or remembered an important appointment.

"What for?" he said, his hands clasped on the table, his eyes searching my face. I had my hands firmly in my lap and I avoided his direct look.

"I was shadowing a CID officer. I'm thinking of joining the force. It seemed a good idea to get a feel of what the job might be like."

"A WPC? My mum was a policewoman."

"Really?" I sat forward, looking interested, hoping to steer him slowly round to police business.

It was a mistake. He leant forward too and, ignoring my question completely, gave me a light peck on the lips.

I held my eyes closed for a moment after the kiss. When I opened them he was looking delighted with himself.

"Yes, she met my dad while they were in Hendon, training." He was moving around in his seat looking excited. He was like a kid who had just got a new toy. It was still in the box and he just couldn't wait to get it out. I was sitting still but inside I was squirming. I just hoped that there was no one around who knew me.

"Didn't you want to be a policeman?" I asked,

taking a sip from my drink.

"No thanks. Roger, my brother, it's more in his line."

"He wants to be a policeman?"

"Ever since he was a little boy. Whenever my dad came home from work Roger wanted to know where his hat was, where his truncheon was. In the end my mum and dad bought him a kiddie's policeman outfit."

His smile had disappeared and he was fiddling with one of his rings.

"Lots of kids dress up," I said, thinking for a moment of myself in a nurse's uniform, a cowgirl's outfit, a Spiderman suit.

"It wasn't just that. He was obsessed with it, my brother, even as a small child. He's still as keen as ever. Spent three years in the army cadets, works out down at the gym, is always talking to my dad about what's going on. He's got it all worked out. He's not like a normal fifteen–year-old kid. It's like a vocation with him."

There was a trace of bitterness in his voice.

"What about you?" I said, disconcerted by his sudden change in mood.

"Me? No, I'm not good at taking orders. That and exams. No, working in casual jobs suits me fine. I've had a lifetime of the police force. I don't want anything to do with it. Now, shall we talk about something else?"

His smile returned and I thought, for the first time, that he wasn't bad-looking; if only he'd stop all the silly clichéd chatter. He reached over again and put his hand on top of mine. I left it there. At least there was a table between us.

When the meal came he chatted about his great love: football.

"I've been supporting West Ham since I was nine."

"Um," I said, fitting a triangle of pizza into my mouth. Football held about as much interest for me as a Latin test paper.

"I've got a season ticket and I go to away matches. You should come to one. You'd enjoy it," he said. He meant it too.

I knew a lot of boys from school who were passionately interested in football. I'd even been out with a couple; an Arsenal supporter and a fanatical Liverpool fan. They talked on and on about this goal or that free kick, about defensive play or the long ball game. They never seemed to notice the glazed, faraway look that settled on my face, the loss of concentration, the stifled yawns.

"Important game, next week," Brian said and I tried to raise my eyebrows to show enthusiasm. "Cup tie. How's your food? Mine's good; garlic bread could have had more garlic though."

"Good," I said.

"The trouble with the Hammers," he went on,

"is they don't spend enough money on players and they depend on the long ball game."

I counted the squares on the tablecloth while he talked on. Occasionally I said, "Um" and nodded.

At least Billy wasn't interested in football. With him it was cars and their parts; the quality of a respray job, the joys of power-assisted steering, the safety features of a Mercedes.

Inexplicably, I felt a pang of guilt thinking of Billy in Norfolk, still annoyed with me for not going with him. What would he say if he could see me there, sitting across the table from Brian Martin like a nodding dog?

Eventually, after what seemed like ninety minutes, he said: "That's enough about me. Let's talk about you."

"There's not much to tell," I said, shrugging my shoulders. I told him a few things and then it went quiet. I glanced at the clock and decided to try and pull Brian back to the topic of conversation that I wanted to talk about.

"Did you know Helen Driscoll?" I said. "The dead girl."

"Not really," Brian said. "I saw her with Roger a few times. I said hello to her once or twice, but I didn't know her."

"What an awful thing to happen. Had your brother been deeply involved with her?"

"He'd gone out with her for a few months. But

she was a bit odd. Anyway, why the interest? It's a bit of a depressing subject."

"Only I spent some time today with the detectives on the case. It's made me curious, you know."

He sat looking at me for a moment. I didn't know whether he was going to oblige me and talk about Helen or whether he was going to kick off on some other subject.

I did the most awful thing. I put my hand across the table and gave his hand a squeeze. As I was doing it a voice inside my head kept shouting at me: *that's going too far; that's not fair.*

"You don't mind talking about it, do you?" I looked him straight in the face, solid eye contact. He really did have rather nice eyes.

"Not at all, *Detective* Kelly," he said and my teeth grated at his feeble attempt at wit. "I need another drink though; how about you?"

When the waitress had brought our drinks he started to tell me about his brother Roger.

"Roger's this really organized, kind of grown-up kid. All his life he's been dead serious. He was completely sold by all the policeman stuff; my dad's radio, his handcuffs, his notebook. He was always asking our mum to take him down the station to see our dad in his uniform, on the front desk or patrolling the streets."

Brian smiled for a second, as though he was

remembering some fond memory.

"My dad was pleased as pie, you know, that his son looked up to him so much. I was never very good at those kinds of things. I got in trouble at the Cubs and couldn't tie knots in the Scouts."

"When did he meet Helen Driscoll?" I asked, steering him back to the subject.

"She was in his year at school and she lived close to us. I don't like to speak ill of the dead, but she was a strange girl."

"Strange?"

"Yes. Moody. Arguing with Roger or her parents. She'd burst into a temper any time, Roger told me. I wasn't surprised when he gave her the push. I wasn't even surprised when she started harassing him. It seemed in character."

"Harassing him?"

"Yes, my dad actually went round to her house, *in uniform*, to warn her off. This was all a while ago. She used to follow Roger and Suzy, his new girl-friend, around. Sometimes she'd shout at them from across the road, saying awful things about Roger. I really thought, at the time, she was a bit unstable. He was a fool to get involved with her in the first place. I'll tell you what, I know it's a bad thing to say, but I'll bet he breathed a sigh of relief when he heard she was dead. Especially since he's started talking about getting engaged. Can you believe it? He's fifteen and he's thinking about marriage! Me, I'm not going to get married until I'm about thirty. Unless I meet the right girl, that is."

He looked straight at me and I felt a ball of panic in my throat.

"Shall we have a sweet?" I said quickly.

It was late when we left the restaurant. He drove me to my street. I knew, on the way, that it would be awkward when he stopped the car, that he would want to kiss me.

I thought, at one point, that it was time to be honest with him: *Look Brian, I like you more than I thought I would, but not in that way. Couldn't we just be friends?*

I kept letting the words play over and over in my head as the car slowed down and the engine hummed to a stop. I was about to open my mouth and say it when he turned across me and put his lips gently on mine.

That was the time to push him away. It wouldn't have been hard. He was near to me but not resting on me. His mouth, open on mine, was barely touching me, yet I felt his hot breath, close and warm. Instead I put my hand up to the back of his head and touched his hair and he kissed me harder.

In the back of my head an excuse was forming: I was tired, I was lonely. I felt grateful towards him. I even quite liked him.

He pulled back and smiled at me. It was a

dangerous moment; he was bound to make some inane comment which would spoil the kiss.

He didn't though. He said: "Come round my house, tomorrow lunch time. My mum and dad will be out. Roger and Suzy will be there. You could meet them."

He scribbled something on a small notepad. "Here's my address."

"OK," I said. I got out of the car.

"See you soon, Patsy Kelly," he said and drove off.

"Yes," I said. I looked at his address: *6 Orchard Drive*. It was round the corner from The Valentines Estate.

12
The Family

Even though it was bitterly cold I decided to walk through The Valentines Estate to get to Brian Martin's house. I went round the edge of the park and turned off the road and past the sign that said: *PRIVATE ROAD RESIDENTS ONLY.* I was only a few metres from the traffic but it seemed quieter. The streets were lined with trees and shrubs and the further I walked the more hushed it became.

The road itself felt different. It took me a minute to work out why. There were no markings; no broken white line down the middle, no yellow lines at the sides. The street lights were smaller, more old-fashioned. There were no cars parked on the road itself, just sleek expensive saloons and hatchbacks sitting side by side in the driveways. Billy would have been interested in exactly what make and type. To me they just suggested wealth; that and the detached, brick-built, solid, two and three storey houses that stood behind them.

I got out my notebook. In among the scribblings I had made from the police station was Helen's address: 8 Park Drive, The Valentines. I walked on, further away from the traffic, into the trees and shrubs. At one point I could no longer see the end of the road and it felt as though I was in the middle of the countryside.

I stood outside number eight. It was almost opposite the house that Billy and I had delivered the yellow Mini to some months before. The down-stairs curtains were still drawn, even though it was past midday. There were no cars in the drive. It looked deserted. I walked on a few metres and stood at a lamp-post, looking at the house. The windows were small and wooden and the glass was leaded. I wondered which one was Helen's bedroom.

How I would have liked to get into her room and look through her stuff; to rummage through her wardrobe, dressing table, maybe a bedside chest of drawers; to sort through her schoolbag and pencil case, a rucksack, a shoulder bag; to dip into the pockets of her clothes, her coats, jackets, jeans; to read the things she had written, her books, her diary maybe, some letters.

I mentally stamped my foot with the frustration

of it; if I were a police detective I would have access to such things. I would be able to talk to all her family and friends, to call at the neighbours, to go to her school, to really find out about her, what she was like and whether she had made any enemies.

Instead I was sidelined. It was like running a race with my feet tied together.

Just then I heard a front door slam. I looked round and saw a young girl come out of the house across the way and walk towards the yellow Mini. I walked quickly across.

"Hello," I said, rubbing my gloved hands together. "How's the car going?"

The girl looked at me quizzically.

"My friend and I delivered your car. In fact it belonged to my friend. He sold it to your mum and dad."

"Oh," she said, looking fondly at the Mini. I noticed then how the paintwork was like a mirror. It had been well looked after. "It's brilliant," she said.

"My friend's a car enthusiast. He buys cars and does them up. He spent weeks on this. I thought he might keep it, he worked so hard on it."

"I'm really pleased with it," she said, still looking at me a little strangely.

"Only I was just coming round to pay my respects to Mrs Driscoll and I noticed it here. She doesn't seem to be at home though."

"You know them?" the girl said warily.

"Yes, my mother and Elizabeth are friends," I said, remembering the name from my notes. "I've been out of the country since Christmas." My mind was racing just slightly ahead of my voice trying to put a story together. "Skiing. I got back yesterday and she told me about it. Awful business."

"Yes," the girl said, relaxing somewhat, "it's upset everyone. The whole family went away because of the press harassment. They were everywhere for days."

"Awful," I said sincerely. "As if the parents haven't been upset enough."

"Her brother had a fight with one of them; smashed his camera."

"Really?" I said, searching for his name inside my head. Eventually it came. "Poor Joe, he must be devastated."

"He was, apparently. It just goes to show you that even adopted brothers and sisters can be close."

"Yes," I said. *Adopted*. It hadn't said anything about that in Helen's file.

"I must go," she said and got into the car. I watched her pull away.

Helen's brother was adopted. I shrugged my shoulders. I had no way of knowing whether that information had any bearing on the case. I just filed it away in the miscellany part of my brain and hoped it would come in useful later.

Brian had the door open as I walked up his pathway.

He had a wide smile on his face, a look of delight that I had arrived, as if he had half expected me not to come. I felt a flood of sympathy for him and resolved to be straight with him, not lead him on any further.

He introduced me to his brother.

"Roger, this is Patsy. She and you should have something in common. She wants to join the police."

"Yes?" Roger said, coming towards me.

Roger Martin was taller than his brother, although clearly younger. He was muscular as well, his shoulders broad. He gave me a firm handshake; a surprisingly confident thing for someone so young to do.

"This is Suzy," he said and pointed to a small blonde girl who was sitting on a chair. She smiled at me but said nothing.

There was an awkward quiet moment when nobody spoke. All sorts of small talk went through my head but it was dwarfed by the real questions that I wanted to ask Roger.

Eventually Suzy said: "Is it still as cold?"

"Yes," I said, moving towards the fire.

"Just as well I made some soup then," Brian said.

"Yes," Roger said, rolling his eyes towards Suzy. Suzy smiled at him and then looked mischievously at me.

"Brian's a really good cook, did he tell you?"

"No," I said, genuinely surprised.

Brian walked round behind me and put his arm loosely round my shoulder. It was a possessive gesture and I felt embarrassed for him. He was clearly building up his hopes on me. It was going to be harder on him when I had to let him down.

"Winter vegetables with Stilton cheese," he said and walked away into the kitchen. I suddenly felt hungry.

Roger dominated the conversation around the table.

"You take the police," he said, "they get the blame for everything. If they're too hard, they get stamped on. If they let people off with a caution, they get pilloried. They can't win!"

Brian was much quieter than he had been the previous evening. He kept cutting up bread and offering the plate of croutons. I ate my soup greedily. I noticed that Roger and Suzy just sipped at theirs, avoided the croutons, and gave each other little secret looks.

"The police force needs women, there's no doubt about that. It has to be said though that women, no matter how bright they are, are simply not as strong as men."

"But – " I said, my mouth full of soup, my spoon in mid-air. My uncle Tony's face came into my head.

"Take a situation like this. It's a Saturday night, you've got a couple of drunks causing trouble, one of them is six foot tall and well built. Are you telling me that an average woman, five six, five seven, could deal with that?"

I opened my mouth to answer but he carried on.

"Of course not. It takes a man in a physical situation like that. Now you're quite well built, Patsy, but look at little Suzy here. How could she deal with that?"

We all looked at Suzy and she gave a silly little smile. She was tiny, four or five inches shorter than me and very thin. Helen Driscoll had been small, Heather had said. Perhaps Roger liked that type; the word "petite" came into my head.

Brian cleared the plates away.

"That was really good!" I said to him, meaning it. He smiled with pleasure and didn't seem to notice the half-full plates he took from Suzy and Roger.

"I was in the station yesterday," I said, trying to direct the conversation towards Helen Driscoll. "Everyone there still seems very involved in the Railway Murders. Of course, Roger, you went out with poor Helen Driscoll. I hope you don't mind, but I was asking Brian about it last night."

"Poor Helen," Roger said, picking up a crouton and popping it into his mouth.

"Was it long ago that you and she finished?"

Roger looked at Suzy.

"The end of the summer," she said and gave his hand a squeeze.

"Brian said it finished badly," I said. "That must

have been awful for you, Suzy."

"You're not kidding," she said and sat forward at the table. It was the first time I had seen her alert. "She never left us alone, did she, Roger? She used to wait for us to come out of school in the afternoon and then follow us home shouting things, horrible, abusive things."

"Poor Suzy," Roger said.

"She tried to spread rumours in school about me, didn't she, Roger?"

"Cake?" Brian put a plate on the table with an oblong cake on it. It was dark and heavy-looking, like a slab of earth.

"Yes, please," I said, unsure. Roger and Suzy both shook their heads.

"It's banana." Brian cut off a piece that was at least three centimetres thick.

"The funny thing was," Roger said, "she wasn't like that when we first broke up. She was quite haughty then. Wouldn't speak to me, ignored me when she saw me. Even when I started seeing Suzy she just went her own way; she started hanging round with that older girl, you know, the kid who moved to Bethnal Green."

"Fay Norris," Suzy said.

"Then suddenly, overnight almost, she got nasty, started with the name-calling."

"And the phone calls. Don't forget those."

"Phone calls?"

"She kept phoning me up, at all hours." Roger was tracing an invisible pattern on the table with his finger. "Threatening, my dad called it. In the end he went round to her house and warned her."

"How awful," I said, breaking off a piece of cake and gingerly putting it into my mouth.

"If you think that's bad, you should hear about the way she treated her brother."

"Her brother?" I said, though my mouth was full.

"Poor Joe, she teased him and made him feel miserable, didn't she, Roger; even when you were going out with her."

"Because he was adopted?" I said.

"She was just plain horrible to him. He wasn't very bright, was he, Roger? And she felt embarrassed, you know. He was in a special slow class and had extra help."

"He's a bit odd-looking as well. Nice bloke – well, I like him."

"He's much bigger than he should be for his age, really good at games and stuff. You took him climbing once, didn't you, Roger? He liked it, was really good at it you said."

"Yes, he was," Roger agreed.

"One of her mates told me that she used to taunt him because he was adopted and she wasn't. She used to tell him that she'd arrange for him to go back into care, didn't she, Roger?"

"Poor Joe," Roger said.

"He didn't really fit into that family at all. After Roger and Helen broke up he spent a lot of time here. Used to hang round Roger's dad, said he wanted to be a policeman."

"My dad took him into the station, just the other week. I haven't seen much of him since then. Nothing since the murder, of course."

"I never liked her," Brian said.

"She never liked your cooking, that's why," Roger said and gave Suzy a sly look.

"I understand that Joe Driscoll is really upset about his sister's death, though."

"Really?" Suzy said, getting up from the table.

"So they said at the station," I lied.

"Don't suppose it'll affect his game though," Roger said.

"Game?"

"Squash. He might not be very bright but he's brilliant at squash. Junior champion down at Valentines sports club. Plays virtually every day."

"You nearly beat him once!" Suzy said, looking up at Roger.

"That's true," Roger said modestly.

After they'd gone we sat on the settee. Brian had the football teletext pages on the screen of the TV but there was no sound. We sat for a while staring at the match scores. Interestingly enough Brian never said a word about football, just talked about other things;

his job in PHOTOKWIK, his car, his plans. Then he started to talk about his mum.

"I'm more like she is really. She hated the police force, left at the first opportunity. She's a caterer now, makes the food for weddings and functions. Sometimes I help her. I suppose that's how I got interested in cooking. My dad doesn't approve, of course; it's not a man's job. Neither does Roger; that must have been clear. No, I don't suppose I'm what you'd call close to my dad. Your parents are divorced, aren't they?"

"Yes, five years ago." I started to tell him about my mum and dad's break-up.

The living room was getting darker although neither of us made a move to put a light on. The fact that the TV was on without any sound made the room seem unnaturally quiet; as if there was a definite absence of noise. It was churchlike; my voice telling a story, him sitting listening, interrupting now and then to ask something.

After a while we both became silent. I glanced at my watch and thought that I ought to go. I was leaning against him on the settee. It was almost dark in the room except for the glow of the TV screen.

"This is nice," he said and rested his hand on my hair.

I knew that it was time to tell him, to be straight with him, to say: *I like you, Brian, but I don't feel attracted to you.*

I didn't though. The strangest thing happened. I sat up and leant over to kiss him. I pressed my lips on his and put my hand into his hair. My eyes were closed and I turned my head to the side and let my tongue touch his teeth.

He sat forward and kissed me again and after a few moments he put his arm around me.

A little voice in my head was asking me what I thought I was doing and the answer was I didn't know. It was warm, it was comfortable. He had made a nice cake and I was lonely.

He suddenly sat up.

"Look at that!" he said. I turned and looked at the screen; West Ham had scored a goal.

I began to laugh, more at myself than anything else.

Brian dropped me off at my house at about six. I said I'd ring him.

When I got in I went straight to my bedroom and wrote down as much as I could remember about what had been said. I made a heading – "ROGER" – and put all the stuff I'd heard under it. I underlined the bit where he had said he'd gone *climbing* with Joe Driscoll. I remembered all the photos of the lengths of rope that had been used to strangle the girls.

The I made another heading – "JOE DRISCOLL" – and wrote down all the information I'd heard; that he was adopted; his sister made his life a misery; he was not very bright but big and fit; he played squash almost every day at The Valentines squash club.

Finally, I wrote the name "FAY NORRIS". Underneath it there was just a blank space. She was someone I had yet to find out about.

Then I closed the book and put it away in a drawer. I really had had enough of it all for one day. I shut the drawer as tightly as I could, as if that might keep it there, out of my head for a few hours.

I kept thinking about Brian Martin though, a vague feeling of guilt lining my stomach. Was I using him? I liked him more that I had before, I especially liked his kisses, but was I being unfair? I knew the answer and it didn't make me feel very good.

I went downstairs with a heavy heart and told my mum I was going to get a video.

"Oh," she said, as I opened the front door, "Billy rang. He's coming back from Norfolk tomorrow."

"Is he?" I said, my spirits suddenly lifted at the thought of seeing him again.

"Yes, he asked where you were. I told him you were out on a date."

"What?" I said with dismay.

"I said you were out with a new boyfriend. That was all right, wasn't it?"

"Oh, hell," I said. The honest truth was I didn't know whether it was all right or not.

13
Joe Driscoll

The next day was Sunday. I put Billy and Brian Martin out of my mind and thought about Joe Driscoll. I rang The Valentines squash club and asked whether the junior champion was playing that day. I said I wanted to watch him for tips on technique. After a bit of paper-rustling the receptionist came back and told me he was playing at two-thirty.

I put the phone down and looked at my watch. I had plenty of time.

I went into the kitchen. My mum was there with her friend Sheila. On the table were several Sunday newspapers laid out. As well as our usual broadsheet papers I noticed a couple of the tabloids as well. Sheila was poring over the details of the Railway Murders.

"Look here, imagine this," she said and started to read out bits. I clicked the kettle back on and waited for it to boil.

"'*COP'S SON'S SWEETHEART LAST VICTIM OF RAILWAY KILLER*'," she went on as my mum looked up from her newspaper. "'*Helen Driscoll, the last victim of the crazed Railway Killer, was romantically linked with the son of a police inspector, it was revealed last night.*'"

So the press had got hold of the story. I only hoped that Des Murray and Stevie didn't think it had been me who had told them.

"It's in here as well," my mum said from behind her giant paper. "'*POLICE INSPECTOR'S DISMAY AT IDENTITY OF VICTIM: Although uniformed inspector John Martin was not directly involved in the Railway Murders investigation, he was shocked and upset when told that the last victim was fifteen-year-old Helen Driscoll. The inspector's son, Roger, had been at school with the girl and the pair had been dating some months previous to the murder.*'"

I looked over her shoulder at the report. There was a small picture of a uniformed officer. Underneath it said: "Inspector Martin". He had a peaked cap on and only a small portion of his face was visible. He looked ordinary; just like any other police officer.

"Look," Sheila said, "here's a picture." She held up her newspaper. It was a school class photograph and the editor had ringed two faces; one was Helen Driscoll's and the other Roger Martin's. Underneath there was a caption: "*Tragic lovers*".

I skimmed the article. It was factually inaccurate, suggesting that the relationship between Roger and Helen Driscoll had still been going on at the time she was killed. I suppose it made a better story. I wondered what Suzy would make of it.

Sheila was immersed in the article. When she'd read it she closed the paper and flicked through the one underneath. In that I could see another angle the journalists had taken: "*I LIVED IN FEAR OF 'RAILWAY KILLER' exclusive by ex-wife Brenda Knight.*"

"Why do you read this stuff, Sheila?" I asked, pouring some boiling water on to a tea bag.

"I like to see what my students are reading," she said, her eyes scanning the pages, her mouth slightly open, her tongue licking her upper lip.

"Sure," I said and looked at my mum, who was hidden from Sheila behind her paper.

She sucked in her cheeks and raised her eyebrows. "Course you do, Sheila," she said.

I'd only been to The Valentines squash club once before. My uncle Tony had asked me to deliver a letter to a solicitor who had been playing a game there.

The club was a two-storey brick building that was

surrounded by a lawn. It was pristine, the windows glittering and not a bit of litter in sight. The doors in the reception were automatic and really did open when you walked up to them.

I had my sports bag with me and poking out of it was the end of my mum's squash racquet. I hoped that I looked like someone coming to play. I'd also put my hair into several small plaits and stuck on a basketball cap that I had. In my pocket I had a large lump of chewing gum that looked like pink play-doh. I was hoping to appear younger than my age.

I walked straight through reception towards the changing-room area and the squash courts. No one stopped me; no one even noticed me.

Once inside the building I looked for the sign that said "Spectators' Gallery". It took me up a flight of stairs.

There were eight squash courts. The spectators' gallery ran between them – four on one side, four on the other. I was above the players, looking down on them. Three of the courts had women playing on them, two had older men and on another two Asian men were playing. On the last one a young boy was playing an older man. The young boy appeared to be winning.

It had to be Joe Driscoll. The boy was big; three or four inches taller than the man he was playing. He looked muscular as well and was quick on his feet. He seemed to fly from one edge of the court to the other. The man he was playing managed to return the ball three or four times before missing it. Then he leant over, his hands resting on his knees. When he stood up his mouth was strained and his face a beetroot colour.

He said something to the boy but I couldn't catch it because of the noise from the other courts. After a few more minutes' play the man picked up a towel that had been in the corner, put it round his head and walked towards the door. The boy followed him and they disappeared into the changing-room area.

I went to the seating area just outside the changing rooms and sat down. I looked at my watch a number of times. After about ten minutes Joe Driscoll appeared at the door. He was dressed and his hair was wet and combed back. I stood up, knowing that if I didn't approach him then, I'd never do it.

I walked away from him at first, then "tutted" to myself and turned round quickly, as though I'd forgotten something from the changing rooms. I deliberately kept my eyes on the ground and allowed myself to walk straight into him. It was quite a collision. My head hit him somewhere in the chest and my bag fell to the ground. My mum's squash racquet slid out and bounced a couple of times on the parquet flooring.

"Oh, no," I said, without looking at him. I retrieved the racquet and stood up apologizing profusely.

"I'm so sorry. I wasn't looking where I was going; did I hurt you? I'm really sorry."

"No, no."

He said the words slowly, completely unflustered. I looked up at him.

"I just don't look where I'm going. I'm always doing this."

I stood looking deep into his face for a few seconds. I got out the chewing gum and poked it into my mouth. I creased my forehead as though I was trying to work something out.

"Don't I know you?" It was a corny thing to say but it was all I had up my sleeve. "You're Helen's brother Joe, aren't you? Joe Driscoll. My God, fancy seeing you after all this time. And in these awful circumstances. Poor Helen. It was so awful."

He was still standing in the same position looking at me. His face didn't give a lot away.

"It's me, Patsy Page. I was in your sister's class at school. I left a couple of years ago. I read about Helen in the paper. It was dreadful."

He stood looking at me unsurely. Close up he looked his age, even though he was bigger than me by about six inches. He had mousy hair and his skin was pale with the stirrings of acne. We had to move out of the way so that a man with a trolley of canned drinks could get to a nearby machine.

"Patsy?" he said, a look of incomprehension on his face.

He didn't believe me. Maybe he thought I was a newspaper reporter. With some panic in my chest I surged on: "I saw Roger Martin a couple of days ago and poor Suzy; they're really upset. I couldn't believe it when I heard. You never think it's going to happen to someone you know, do you?"

"No," he said, softening a bit at the mention of Roger and Suzy.

A couple and their children passed us by and we had to move up against the wall.

"I was just going for a cold drink," I said. "Why don't you come?" I looked him straight in the eye, hoping somehow to mesmerize him into joining me. He avoided eye-contact though and I thought I'd lost the gamble. But after a few seconds he shrugged his shoulders and said: "OK."

We went to the far end of the cafeteria. I bought the drinks and as I paid for them I watched him sitting at a table. He seemed unperturbed about being there. A couple of people passed him by and said hello and he nodded in reply, all the time with his eyes averted. It wasn't just me he was avoiding looking at.

I chatted for a while, making up stories about me and Helen Driscoll, and then talked about my new school. He didn't say much, I wasn't even sure that he was listening. I was getting nowhere. After about ten minutes I decided to get to the point.

"Poor Helen. It must be over a year since I last saw her and now it's too late. How are you coping, Joe? And your mum; Elizabeth, isn't it? She's grief-stricken, I suppose."

I looked up from my drink and caught a fleeting expression on his face. I couldn't have said exactly what it meant because it faded so quickly. His eyelids had closed with irritation and his lips had stretched across his teeth. Then his face just slipped back as it had been: blank.

"And you Joe, I know you and Helen didn't always get on that well, but I bet it's hit you badly as well."

I looked straight at him, caught his eye for a mini-second, then he looked away, at his cup, at the table, anywhere but at me.

"I'll tell you what though, Helen was really fond of you, she was always talking about you; Joe this, Joe that."

"Don't make me laugh!" he said and rolled his eyes.

"Oh, she was, Joe," I continued.

"Helen never cared for anyone but herself."

He said the words distinctly but slowly. He was looking down at his fingers, using his thumbnail to push at his cuticles.

"I know she used to rib you, Joe, but it was never serious…" I said, feeling uneasy about opening this up with someone who was clearly unconfident and ill at ease. What if he was innocent? Did I have the right to upset him like that?

"You weren't there," he said. He turned round to his bag and I had the feeling that he wasn't going to stay there much longer.

"No, but Helen always said…"

"'You're not really part of this family,' she said to me. 'Mum got *paid* for looking after you.'" He put on a high voice when pretending to be Helen.

Then he looked me straight in the face, his eyes locking on mine for a few seconds. I could see he was angry.

"She was proud of your squash-playing," I continued, grabbing at straws.

"She didn't care about anyone but herself. She might have fooled you into thinking… You ask Fay Norris…" He lost his thread and unzipped his bag. He rummaged around for a few minutes and then said: "I sorted her out though, didn't I?"

"What do you mean?" I said.

"I sorted her out. I put her right."

His hands were flat on the table. Close up I noticed how big they were, his fingers thick and powerful.

"Helen?"

"'Oh Joe, how could you be so horrible,'" he mimicked her voice again. Then lowered his voice: "I sorted her out."

He stood up, towering above me, his hands

hanging heavily for a moment; then picked up his bag and said: "I've got to go."

I watched him walk out. A number of people at other tables were looking at him, nudging each other. Whether it was because he was the junior squash champion or had a murdered sister, I didn't know.

14
Visitors

When I got home the house was empty. There was a note on the kitchen table: *Gone to cinema, be back about eight, love Mum.*

I got out my notebook and wrote down as much as I could remember of what Joe Driscoll had said. I even tried to put his exact words down: *She didn't care about anyone but herself... You ask Fay Norris... I sorted her out.*

I pulled the plaits out of my hair and looked in the fridge for something to eat. I got out some cheese and made a sandwich.

There were two young men, Roger Martin and Joe Driscoll, who both had reasons for disliking Helen. One of them, her adopted brother Joe, hated her.

They both had links with the police station, although Roger's was much stronger than Joe's. Roger wanted to be a policeman, often spent time with his dad talking about the job; surely something as serious as the Railway Murders would have cropped up in conversation, the fact that it was called "Operation Rose". *Why's that? Oh, the murderer left roses on the dead bodies.* Maybe that was why the rose was the wrong colour. Only half the information had got through.

I sat, feeling uneasy about this; Roger Martin simply didn't look the type. Then I pictured Joe Driscoll sitting opposite me in the squash club, his muscular shoulders and arms, his giant hands that seemed to fill the table, his eyes shifting here and there, unable to look me in the face.

Inspector Martin had taken him recently to visit the police station. Like me, maybe he had had a look round, wandered into the conference room. Perhaps he saw the words from a distance, written on the white board, "OPERATION ROSE", glanced at the photographs of the bodies, the roses. Perhaps he was quicker than people gave him credit for. *You can't go in there, son,* Inspector Martin may have said, *that's the nerve centre for the Railway Murders, highly confidential.*

Perhaps, perhaps, perhaps. I picked up my sandwich and bit into it just as the doorbell rang. I carried it out to the front door with me.

It was Billy.

My mouth was full of bread and cheese and it was a minute before I could speak. Usually he would have just walked past me, straight into my kitchen. He didn't though. He stood waiting for me to beckon him in. Eventually, after I'd finished my bite, I said, "Nice to see you," and immediately regretted it. It sounded false and anyhow we usually didn't bother with such niceties. He followed me through to the kitchen and I clicked the kettle on again.

"Tea?" I said and he nodded.

"Good journey?" I said and he nodded.

After a further few seconds of saying nothing he looked at my notes, lying across the table and said:

"So you're carrying on with it, Detective Kelly?"

I stiffened at the tone of his voice. He was mocking me and my unimportant work.

"Billy, if you're annoyed about something come out and say it. And yes, as a matter of fact, I am continuing with the investigation."

I had my hands on my hips and my tongue was pushing against the back of my teeth. For the first time I noticed a brown paper bag that he had on his lap.

"So let the police deal with it. It's their job."

"But ... but what if..."

"What if you're wrong? You're not sure then!"

"I am sure."

"But you don't want to look an idiot. For

123

destroying the photos, for not going to them before now."

"I don't know."

"You want all the glory. After the Judy Hurst case you want to be the centre of attention again." Billy was sitting forward in his seat.

I pulled out a chair and sat down. "No, I don't know," I said miserably.

There was silence for a moment.

"I bought you this," he said abruptly, in the same tone that he'd just been arguing in. He handed me the brown paper bag.

It was a pottery vase.

"Thanks," I said, feeling awkward. We didn't usually buy each other gifts; it was strictly Christmas and birthdays with us. I placed it on the table and he put his hand out and caught my wrist. I looked up at him and without a word he pulled me across and started to kiss me.

I was leaning across the tiny kitchen table. Billy's hands were holding my arms, pulling my mouth on to his. I was still tense from the argument and the angle was uncomfortable. After a few seconds I stopped noticing.

He drew back for a moment and looked at me. I thought he was going to speak but he didn't and I went round the table, sat in the chair next to him and kissed him hard on the mouth, my fingers on his face.

Somewhere in the back of my head I heard a nagging sound. Billy's hands were on my shoulders, one of them running up and down my arm, sending a shiver across my chest.

The nagging noise continued and after another moment I drew back, my mouth wet, and realized that it was the front doorbell.

I got up, smoothing my hair down and walked along the passageway, my head still slightly dazed, wondering what on earth Billy and I were going to say to each other. It had been over a year since we had first kissed. Were we going to be able to talk about it? Refer to it?

I opened the front door. Brian Martin was standing there. Dismay must have been written all over my face because he said: "Don't look so pleased to see me, Miss Patsy Kelly, I'm not stopping, just passing," and then, without another word, he gave me a hug.

I'd turned slightly as he came in, and over his shoulder I could see Billy, standing at the kitchen door watching me. I tried to make a face, to signal that I wasn't enjoying or hadn't asked for such an affectionate display, but my mouth was pushing into Brian's coat and my arms were pinned to my side.

Eventually, after what seemed like ages, he let me go. Billy had disappeared from sight. I heard a sound from the kitchen, as though something had fallen over. Billy appeared, buttoning up his coat.

He walked towards us along the hall.

"I must go, Patsy," he said, ignoring Brian.

"Not on my account," Brian said, looking a little disconcerted as Billy brushed past him.

"My friend Billy," I said, holding my hand out weakly.

"Hi," Brian said, as the front door banged shut. I turned and walked down the hall towards the kitchen.

"Your friend was in a hurry," I could hear Brian's voice from behind me.

In the kitchen, on the floor, were the pieces of the vase that Billy had bought for me.

I felt like crying.

Later, when Brian had gone, I thought about Billy's kiss and the way he had left in a huff as soon as Brian had arrived. Did that mean something *real* was happening between us? I put my hand on my shoulder and rubbed it up and down my arm the way that Billy had done, letting a picture of it come back into my mind.

Did I want something to happen between us?

It was perplexing and I began to sort through my stuff when I heard the front doorbell ring again.

When I opened the door Heather Warren was standing there. I immediately tensed, a feeling of guilt developing, even though I wasn't sure what I had to feel guilty about.

"Patsy," she smiled, "we need to talk."

"Really?" I said, full of innocence.

"About Helen Driscoll, Patsy."

"Oh," I said and held the front door open. She took off her coat and handed it to me. Then she walked past me towards the kitchen. I hung her coat over the banister and hurried after her, wondering what on earth she wanted to see me about.

"A coffee would be good," she said and took a packet of cigarettes out of a bag.

"Milk?" I said timidly. I tidied up the table, tucking my notebook under a pile of magazines.

"Absolutely not, no sugar either," she said and lit up. I silently hoped my mum wouldn't arrive home and find her kitchen full of smoke. I scurried round making the coffee and talking about the weather, the weather and the weather.

Eventually I placed a mug of boiling coffee in front of her. A splash of the liquid came over the side and landed on my hand. It felt like molten liquid. I rubbed the spot with my fingers.

Heather sat looking at me crossly, then picked up the cup and took a mouthful. The steam divided around her face. She never flinched as the liquid went into her mouth. She held it there for a few seconds and then swallowed.

"Lovely," she said and I swallowed a mouthful of saliva. I sat down and forced myself to speak.

"What did you want to see me about, Heather?"

"Well, let me see. Yesterday one of my officers came to see me because a neighbour of Helen Driscoll's parents phoned and said that a strange girl went round to see the family yesterday. The girl was hanging around, asking questions, said her mother knew Mrs Driscoll and so on.

"The neighbour phoned Mrs Driscoll but she knows no one at all fitting the description. The visitor was about your age, Patsy, and had glasses and an unusual hat on."

I sat very still, said nothing. There was no proof that it had been me.

"Then today, not half an hour ago, another of my officers came and told me about a phone call from Mrs Driscoll herself saying that her son, Joe, had been approached by a young girl claiming to be a friend of the late Helen. This girl was not unlike you, Patsy, and guess what? Said her name was Patsy something."

"I…" I started to speak.

"No, no, Patsy. Don't say anything, let me finish. At that very moment my colleague Des Murray was round and he said that when you spent time with him you were very inquisitive about the Railway Murders, about Operation Rose in fact. Now why would that be?"

"I… It's just that…" I blustered, not knowing which words, if any, were going to come out of my mouth next.

"No, no, Patsy, let me finish." She stopped for a moment and took another mouthful of the scalding coffee. "Thing is, I know you're a good detective. I know that because of the Judy Hurst case. I know how enthusiastic you are, Patsy, but the trouble with this investigation is that it's already been solved! We have the murderer. He's on remand, behind bars. You don't have to solve this one, Miss Nancy Drew, it's already been done."

"Right," I said, nodding, as though I'd accepted my telling-off. I looked down at my lap, then at my hands, then back at Heather.

"What's happening, Patsy? I want to know it all."

I sat very still for a moment, then it started to come out. The whole thing: the photographs in the precinct; recognizing the girl; the day at the police station; the contact with Roger Martin; the meeting with Joe Driscoll.

She listened to me without speaking. She lit up three cigarettes, one after the other. When I'd finished, I sat back and looked at her.

"Is that it?" she said.

I nodded and she stubbed out her last cigarette.

"Why didn't you come and tell me, as soon as you recognized the girl?"

"Because I'd thrown the photos away. I had no proof!"

"But I'd have listened to you, Patsy. We could have checked it out. Asked the girl who was sitting in the square to come forward. We could have sorted it."

"But she can't come forward, Heather. She's dead. It was Helen Driscoll. I'm as sure as I can be."

"Then you should have come to me! What did you think you could do? All you've managed to do is upset the Driscolls and they've been upset enough already."

She had raised her voice.

"But Heather," I said, "did you widen your investigations at all, around Helen Driscoll?"

"No, the MO was the same as for the other victims. Why should we? We caught the guy red-handed."

"Both these boys, Roger and Joe, had strong animosities towards Helen."

"But that doesn't mean they killed her!"

"But did you even ask them where they were on the afternoon that she was killed?"

"No, because we have the murderer, in custody." She let out a sigh, as if I was being a nuisance. There was an angry silence. Eventually she said: "What about if I personally find out what these two boys were doing when Helen was killed. You can call it an alibi if you like. When we find out that they had nothing to do with it, will you be satisfied then? Will you drop it then?"

I heard the front door open.

"Yes, of course. I was only…"

The kitchen door opened and my mother came in, Sheila behind her.

"Mum, this is Heather Warren," I said. "Inspector Warren."

My mum smiled but her nose crinkled up and her eyes focused on the plate on the table with the cigarette-ends. Then she looked at me questioningly.

"Heather's just popped by to give me a message for Tony," I said, as though I'd been asked a question.

Sheila came round, her eyes glittering.

"Inspector Warren, of the Railway Murders? Oh, I am pleased to meet you..."

I looked at Heather and raised my eyebrows. She smiled at Sheila.

"I'll be off now, Patsy. Nice to meet you," she said and drained the cooled coffee from her cup. I took her to the front door.

"I'll ring you tomorrow evening. Remember, no more detective work on the Driscoll case, right?" she said in a loud whisper, a glance over my shoulder at the kitchen.

I nodded my head and watched her go off to her car.

15
Fay Norris

I tried to take my mind off the case at work the next day. I spent all morning tidying out the filing cabinets and threw out a lot of dead paperwork. Tony asked me to get out his diary and write in some meetings he had arranged for himself. I noticed that he was meeting Heather Warren on Wednesday morning.

"Why are you meeting Heather?" I said, curious. I knew how much he disliked her.

He was filing his nails and blowing on them. Suddenly I noticed how dark his hair looked, almost jet-black. My aunt Geraldine had been colouring the grey again.

"I'm looking into an old missing persons case. The police and I may be able to help each other. Anyway, now that she's been promoted, I ought to get to know her a bit better. I thought of taking a gift. A box of chocolates? Some flowers?"

He really was serious.

"Would you do that if it was a man?" I said, handing him his diary.

"That's it," he said half-joking, "bring women's rights into everything."

"We are half the population," I said.

"The prettier half, by far," he said. He had a smirk on his face. It was his bull-fighting look. He was going to wave a red rag at me until I charged at him. I wasn't in the mood for playing.

"I'm going to lunch," I said.

"By the way," I could hear his voice as I walked into my office, "how did the date with young Brian go?"

"Never you mind," I shouted.

Brian Martin. He was another thing I was trying not to think about.

Late in the afternoon I got out my notebook and had a flick through. I wondered how long it would take Heather to find out the alibis. I looked at all my work; blocks of writing, lists, words circled and underlined. At the top of a page I noticed the name "FAY NORRIS". Underneath it there was nothing. I took my pen and wrote "BETHNAL GREEN". It was about four stops on the main line into Liverpool Street.

It could take Heather ages to get back to me. She was a busy woman, probably had dozens of other cases to attend to. It could be days or even the end of the week before she rang me.

I made a decision.

It didn't take me long to ring the six Norrises in the phone book. I asked for Fay each time. Only on the last call did I get the answer I wanted: *Fay's not in from college yet. She'll be in at about six.* I copied down the address from the phone book. If only everything else in the case had been as easy to find out as that had been.

I went straight from work to Bethnal Green. I had Fay Norris's address in my bag and an A–Z of London.

I told myself I wasn't really investigating anything, just clearing up some loose ends. All I'd heard about Helen Driscoll had been bad stuff. I wanted to see if her friend had another story to tell.

I walked up her street and decided that I was going to be honest with Fay Norris; no more dramatics, pretending to be a long-lost friend of the family. If she refused to speak to me, then I'd have to leave it at that.

A young woman opened the door of the address that I had. She was older than I had expected, about eighteen. She had long blonde hair, the type you see in the TV ads for hair shampoo.

"Fay Norris?" I asked.

"Yes?" She peered out into the dark street, looking first one way and then the other.

"My name's Patsy Kelly. I work for a private investigations company and I'm doing some personal research on Helen Driscoll. I'd very much like to talk to you."

She frowned at me for a moment and then, pushing the front door to, she said:

"Are you with the newspapers? I've got nothing to say."

I put my hand against the door to stop it closing.

"I'm not a reporter, Fay. Look, I think I was one of the last people to see her before she was murdered. It's sort of important to me to know what she was like." It was honest, even if it didn't tell her everything.

She stood for a minute, her hand playing with the straw-coloured hair.

"You'd better come in," she said.

We went up to her bedroom which was right at the top of the house. It was a small attic room with a bed in the corner and an easy-chair by the tiny window. I looked out and saw the beginnings of splashes of rain on the window. I heard Fay calling something downstairs and then she came into the room.

I sat on the chair and she sat on the bed.

"I wasn't really close friends with Helen, I wasn't

even in the same year. It was just that before we moved here we used to live close to her and she and I walked to school in the mornings. I don't think she had many friends. I kind of felt sorry for her. What do you want to know about her?" she said.

"Why don't I tell you what I know. Then you can fill in anything that's been left out."

"OK." She lay back against the wall and I began to talk. She looked away from me and plaited the ends of her hair, letting it come undone and then starting again. Once or twice she shook her head at something I said but most of the time she just lay, lifting her leg occasionally to look at something on her foot. When I'd finished she sat up and said: "It doesn't surprise me that Roger and Joe should talk about Helen like that. She wasn't always that easy to get on with."

The door of the room opened unexpectedly and a woman brought in a tray with two china cups and saucers on it.

"Some tea for your friend, Fay," the woman said.

"Oh, Mum, there was no need." Fay stood up and took the tray, then gave her mum a hug. The woman went out humming a tune and Fay offered me a cup.

"Helen wasn't happy in that family. At least she had been until Joe came. He was fostered, as you know, then adopted. He was ten when he first went to live there and had enormous problems, learning difficulties I think they called it. Helen said her mum and dad stopped being interested in her. They just became obsessed with the boy, Joe. I think she was exaggerating, you see what I mean?" Fay left the words in mid-air, then drank some of her tea.

"She started to see Roger Martin I suppose about a year ago, maybe not so long, I'm not sure. Anyway, she was dead happy when he started to go out with her. I never knew what she liked about him, he was a real bore...

"Things were all right between them, I think, but I didn't see that much of her then, I was hanging round with some other kids. I'll tell you what though; it was common knowledge that Suzy Peters had her eye on Roger Martin. She started to hang around with their set long before Helen and Roger split up. She was always there, Helen told me, being nice to Roger: 'Isn't that right, Roger? Don't you think so, Roger?' Everyone noticed it."

I smiled, remembering Suzy's way of including Roger's opinion in her conversation.

"I was away when it finished, on holiday I think. There'd been a big party down at the council estate. Helen said something bad had happened; she wouldn't go into it. I assumed she'd caught Roger and Suzy; like I said, we weren't that close then. I was about to move, you see what I mean?"

"She came to visit you though," I said.

"Yes, things started to get much worse at home.

She started to get into trouble at school. She began to bunk off. I'd frequently come out of college in the afternoon and find her there, waiting for me."

"Is that when she began to torment Joe, about him being adopted?"

"No, no," she said impatiently, "she and Joe always had a kind of mickey-taking about that. She'd say he was the new kid in the family, tell him not to get on his high horse. It was a joke, you see what I mean? At least it started that way. I think it got worse in the autumn though. Joe started getting upset about it and instead of leaving it she became serious about it too. Who does he think he is? she'd say. It got worse after Roger dumped her, much worse."

I was getting a different picture of Helen Driscoll. She was mixed up, confused. Someone who had lost her way.

"What about her parents," I said, "didn't they notice?"

"No, it was Joe they focused on, not Helen. Helen was the stable one, the one who could cope; Joe wasn't."

"And Helen was their own daughter, more secure than the adopted boy," I said.

Fay was silent and looked at me for a minute. Then she said: "Helen made me promise not to tell anyone but now, I suppose, it doesn't matter." She shrugged her shoulders. "Helen and Joe were rowing all the time. Helen told me that one afternoon she was really unpleasant to him. She came round here and said, 'I've gone too far, Fay, I've really upset Joe.' She said she was going to go home and make it up to him.

"I didn't expect to see her for a while but she was outside my college, the next afternoon. She was in a terrible state. I brought her home here and she told me everything. It seems that Joe was so upset with her taunting that he went to their mother and told her. Mrs Driscoll was furious and called Helen in. She told Helen then and there, that Joe hadn't been the only adopted child, that she, Helen, was also in fact adopted."

I didn't say anything. It was a piece of information I hadn't expected.

"Apparently the Driscolls had adopted Helen at birth. They'd never told her, thinking they'd never need to. But the adoption people asked them to have Joe, and he'd had such an awful life that they'd taken him. He knew he was adopted but they couldn't suddenly tell Helen. She was ten, after all. So they just left things the way they were."

"So Helen found out that she was just the same as Joe."

"Yes, it changed her. She became really bitter towards them, you see what I mean? She seemed to hate everyone. That's when she started to get nasty towards Roger and Suzy."

"Oh."

"She stopped coming to see me for a while. She started to write me letters. Here, I'll get you the last one she sent, just before Christmas."

Fay got up off the bed and went to a small chest of drawers. She pulled out a small envelope and gave it to me.

Dear Fay, [it said] *just two weeks to Christmas and I'm almost there. I've found out that my real mum and dad both come from north London; the adoption agency have suggested that I write my mother a letter through them. Maybe she will want to see me.*

Things are just the same at home, Joe is walking round like he owns the place. My mum and dad are still angry at me for the way I treated Joe. I can't blame them.

Everywhere I go I see Roger and Suzy. They make me sick. Everybody thinks he's such an angel. If only they all knew him like I do.

Hope all is well with you, I'll try to get over before Christmas. Love, Helen.

"She was looking for her natural mother?" I said.

"Yes, had been ever since her mum, Mrs Driscoll, told her."

"I wonder if that's why Joe Driscoll was so cocky about Helen when I spoke to him." I remembered his words: *I sorted her out.*

"Joe was always dead odd."

"So she was adopted too," I said quietly to myself. I wondered if it meant anything. The

140

window was glistening with raindrops. Every few minutes I could hear a bus splashing along the wet street outside.

"She wasn't all bad, you know," Fay said. "She had a kind heart, but you know lately she just seemed bad-tempered all the time and when she found out about her parents, well..." Fay held her palms upwards and shrugged her shoulders. I stood up, handed her back her letter and walked downstairs. When I got to the front door she said:

"When you saw her, you know, before that maniac got her, how did she look? Did she look happy?"

I thought about it for a minute, remembering Helen's rigid face, her slumped posture, her stare, through the playground, through me. I opened my mouth to speak.

"It's OK," Fay said, using her hands to pull her long yellow hair back behind her ears. "You don't have to say. I can guess what she was like."

I got home at about eight. There was a message on the answer-phone from Heather.

"This is for Patsy. I'll be brief; if you want to ring me for more details I'll be in the office in the morning. Roger Martin was in school on the afternoon of the tenth of January, taking internal exams; mathematics, I believe. Joe Driscoll was absent from school because he was playing in the local semi-finals of the under-sixteen's squash championships.

Like I said, I'm here in the morning if you want to go over it. Bye-bye."

It was all a dead-end. My murder victim had turned out to be quite different from what I had thought and my two suspects, Roger Martin and Joe Driscoll, had cast-iron alibis.

Maybe Heather had been right. I should have dropped the case.

16
Relatives

I had my lunch the next day in the precinct where I had last seen Helen Driscoll alive. Billy was going to meet me there. It was cold and icy but I sat with a packet of chips on the same bench that I had sat on the day I was following Mr Black.

Tony had given me the afternoon off. Business was slack and he said he was going to meet some of his insurance friends.

There were a number of schoolkids lounging around the playthings in the square. A boy of about fourteen was on a tiny swing and some loud girls were sitting flicking sand at each other. Everywhere there was debris from the chip shop; bits of paper, chips thrown away carelessly on the pavement. I began to feel very old, wishing the teenagers could just use the bins.

Billy turned up at about one. He took a chip and said: "What's happening? Why are we meeting here?"

"I just thought, now that it's all over, you might like to see where it all happened, where I saw Helen Driscoll."

"It's all over?" he said and looked at me. He knew what I meant but there was a mischievous look in his eye, as though he was referring to the events of Sunday evening. Maybe I was just being too sensitive.

"Heather Warren came, after you left. She gave me what you might call a major telling-off."

Billy raised his eyebrows. Looking down at my knees I told him about Heather's comments and her phone call the previous evening informing me of the alibis. From time to time I lifted my head to look at him but his head was turned away, or his eyes were fixed on some point in the middle distance. I also told him about my visit to Fay Norris.

"So Helen Driscoll's life gets more mysterious at every turn," he said unexpectedly. He sounded serious. A small surge of hope rose in my chest. He looked me straight in the eye for the first time. I couldn't help but think of the kiss. It sat there between us, huge and unmentionable.

"Yes," I said.

"And you're absolutely sure it was her you saw here on this bench at two thirty-two." He had adopted a businesslike voice, as if he was on the brink of suing someone.

"Absolutely. Utterly. Without any doubt."

"But it looks like the boyfriend and the brother are definitely not involved."

"It looks that way," I said grudgingly, still not completely convinced. He had leaned back on the bench and his shoulder was touching mine.

"If you're right, and she was here at the time that Leslie Knight was caught, there's only one other explanation. Someone else killed her for some other reason."

"Um…" It was unlikely; even someone as mixed up and difficult as Helen couldn't have had that many enemies.

"Let's go through it all again, from the beginning."

I was surprised. There wasn't a hint of sarcasm in Billy's voice. I wondered what he was up to. Had he decided to humour me, let me get it all out of my system the way a parent would go along with a child, or was he genuinely interested? Either way I needed the audience.

I leant back and started at the beginning again; the photographs, the realization that it had been Helen I had seen. I got out my notebook and told Billy about my day with CID, my trip with Heather to the place where Helen's body had been found.

Billy took the book and flicked through the pages

asking me about the notes: What's Operation Rose? Who's Inspector Martin? Who said the words: *Helen, you should have got to know me better*?

I told him about the evening with Brian Martin (omitting the kisses) and my meeting with Roger and his girlfriend Suzy. Finally there was Joe Driscoll's story; the rest he knew.

We sat, idly flicking through my notebook, as though the answer might jump up out of a page. I looked round the precinct and noticed that the schoolchildren had gone; the swing was hanging listlessly and the sand was deserted; an empty can of Coke was rolling down the incline towards the shops.

The man from the chip shop had come out and was gathering up some of the bits of paper and rubbish left by the schoolchildren. Just along, past Majestic Dry Cleaner's, outside the Asian shop, I noticed a bucket full of cut flowers that were for sale. It reminded me of the sad bouquets that had lined the pavement outside the railway warehouses where Helen had been found. The words, *Helen, you should have got to know me better*, kept going through my head, like the chorus of a song.

Finally Billy spoke.

"You know there's something important that you've left out of all this."

"What?" I said, mildly miffed. Over the last few days I'd covered a lot of ground, even though it had left me in the middle of nowhere, quite literally back where I had started.

"You saw her here, in the square, on her own, right?"

"Yes."

"When kids bunk off school they usually do it with mates. They do it to be with their mates, right?"

"Mostly, yes."

"But she was here, on her own."

"Yes." I couldn't see what Billy was getting at. My attention was taken by the Asian woman, coming out of the shop and picking up one of the bunches of flowers. I watched as she shook the water from the bottom of it before taking it inside the shop.

"So perhaps she was here, on this bench, for some particular reason."

"What though?" Why should a cold bench in the middle of a tatty square of shops hold any clue to Helen's death?

"Thing is," Billy sat forward, "remember that girl in the year above us, at school, Rosemary someone? The kid who had been in care; you know, the one who arrived in the social worker's car every day."

"Rosemary Lewin?"

"Yes. I heard, I can't remember exactly when, but I heard that she'd started to look for her real mother."

I didn't say anything.

"I heard that she'd found her through some agency or other. The thing is she went to see the woman and..."

"It was awful, I remember, the woman didn't want to know her."

"That's right. The woman had a family of her own, a husband; I can't remember exactly but the point is that she didn't want Rosemary around."

"Helen Driscoll was looking for her mother, Fay Norris said; in fact she was close to finding her; it said so in a letter that I read."

"Exactly," Billy said. He opened the pages of the notebook and went on: " *'Helen, you should have got to know me better.'* What if that bouquet was from her natural mother?"

"You think her mother killed her?" I said incredulously.

"No," Billy said, exasperated, "but it might explain why she was here, in this square. If someone else knew that Helen was here that would back up your story. The police might reopen the investigation."

I had a blank look on my face, but in my head a picture was moving into focus. I remembered Helen sitting on the bench, her body relaxed, her head rigid, as if she were *looking at something*. She had been staring past me, preoccupied even when the toddler fell over.

I looked round and saw Majestic Dry Cleaner's. I

remembered the day I had been there, my camera in my bag. There had been a woman, in a grey overall, looking out on to the square, at the same moment that Helen had been looking in.

I stood up and grabbed Billy's arm.

"My God," I said, "she was here, in this square, because it was where she'd found her mother. That's why she was sitting on the bench, staring into that shop." I pointed to the dry cleaner's.

"Don't get too excited. It's just a guess," Billy said.

But it wasn't. I felt suddenly that it was right. That it had been staring me in the face. Helen had no other connection to that square. It was miles from her school and she had no friends there.

Helen, you should have got to know me better. The note must have been from her mother.

"Maybe there's some connection with all this and her murder," I said, excitement sizzling through me. Billy put his hand on my arm.

"Patsy, slow down. Take it one step at a time. You can't go rushing in accusing people of murder."

"I know, I know. What do you take me for?"

"We'll have to think of some way to find out, without asking the woman straight out. What if her family's there?"

"She may not want everyone to know that she's Helen's mother."

"Slow down, take it easy. We won't rush into it."

We walked towards the dry cleaner's, talking

quietly. Just before I opened the door I squeezed Billy's arm and whispered:

"Billy, you're brilliant. You've cracked this case."

The heat from the dry cleaner's hit us as we walked in the door. It was a relief to be out of the cold but it quickly became oppressive. We waited for a moment while the woman behind the counter served someone else.

She looked familiar, not unlike my own mum, perhaps a bit older. She had a short grey overall on over jeans. Her dark hair was hanging round her face and she had no make-up on. She looked hot and red-faced. She had glasses on that had slipped down to the end of her nose; every few seconds she pushed them back up again with her middle finger. She talked constantly to the woman she was serving, about the weather, the price of apples and the government. When the woman left with her dry cleaning she said, "I'll just be a minute and then I'll be with you." She walked into the back of the shop and I could hear her talking to someone. A male voice answered indistinctly and then she came out again, carrying an armful of clothes on hangers and, puffing slightly, she laid them down on a section of the counter.

I noticed then, with a flicker of concern, that she was not at all like Helen; she was much bigger, taller and broader. What had I hoped for? That she would be Helen's double? Only twenty years older?

"Now." She held out her hand and looked expectantly, first at me, then at Billy. I realized after a second that she was waiting for our dry cleaning ticket. Billy spoke:

"Sorry to bother you, only our friend left her dry cleaning in here the other week and we've come to pick it up. We've got no ticket though."

"Oh," the woman said, pulling a giant, dog-eared book out from under the counter. "Name?"

Billy looked at me; I held my breath.

"Her name was Helen Driscoll; D.R.I.S.C.O.L.L. It was about a week ago. She lived on The Valentines estate."

The woman's head was bent over the book. Her eyebrows crinkled for a moment and she continued to point her finger on the page and move it downwards.

"About a week ago?" she said, turning back through the book.

I looked closely at her, to see if there was even a flicker of recognition at Helen's name, but there was nothing. I decided to push it further.

"Yes, it's very sad. Our friend was killed last week, murdered I should say."

"How awful," the woman said, looking at me, then at Billy. She used her finger to push up her glasses. "Driscoll, did you say? I'm sure I haven't got any dry cleaning here under that name. I'll just check in the back. I don't work here all the time, only part-time you see; my husband might remember something."

She disappeared for a minute and I could feel disappointment beginning to lean on my shoulders. Billy was looking round the shop, avoiding my look.

"No, I'm sorry," she said from the back, her voice reaching us before she did, "my husband doesn't remember anything about it. I'm so sorry. Do you thing it might have been another dry cleaner's?"

We said yes, probably, and left the shop, hearing the "ting" of the door as it shut behind us.

"Maybe it wasn't the dry cleaner's," Billy said. "Maybe it was one of the other shops."

We looked around but there was only the Asian grocery, the Chinese fish and chip shop and the car parts place that was over on the far side. I had distinctly remembered Helen looking to my right and that was where the dry cleaner's was.

My memory. It was the only thing holding me on to this case. It was like a thin thread that was being pulled and stretched and was at breaking point.

"I've got to go and deliver a car this afternoon. Why don't I run you back home?" Billy said. I must have looked suicidal because he put his arm round my shoulder in a big-brother hug. I followed him round the corner to the car, a black hatchback with a crumpled side-wing.

"I'm taking it to get it priced for an insurance

job," Billy said, opening the door. He stopped mid way, looking past me, towards the precinct. I turned round. A man was walking towards us. I stood still as he came closer. He was tall and very thin. He was wearing a grey overall, the arms of which were too short. He stopped and said nothing; then looking as though he had just made a decision he said:

"Can I talk to you?" He clasped his hands and I noticed his bony wrists and knuckles, the skin only just seeming to cover the long fingers. "It's about what you said, in the dry cleaner's. It's about Helen Driscoll. I knew her, you see. No, be perfectly honest," he seemed to be talking to himself, "she came to see me last week. She's..." He stopped speaking for a moment, then lowered his voice. "She says she's my daughter. That I'm her father. That I *was* her father."

17
Daughter

We drove away from the precinct with the man in the back of the car. We parked a couple of streets away. He talked most of the time.

"My name's Ron Carpenter. My wife, you see, she doesn't know anything about this. Sarah, my wife, would be very upset. She has no idea that I have a daughter at all. That's why I've not contacted anyone, the police..."

He had one of his hands over the back of my seat. It sat there, almost touching me, pale and skeletal. I moved closer to the window.

When we pulled up he stopped talking and took an inhaler out of his pocket. He sucked on it and after holding his breath for a few minutes he said, "She just turned up one day and said, 'Hello, Dad', bold as brass."

He kept looking out of the car windows, up and down the street we were parked in.

"My wife and I, we've been running the dry cleaner's for about five years now. We've no children of our own. My wife couldn't have them. It's one of the reasons why I don't want Sarah to know."

"But did you see Helen, there in the park, on the day she was murdered?" I said, remembering my hope that he would back up my story.

"On the day she died? You mean the Tuesday? The day she went missing? No, no. I'm sure I didn't. I was at the wholesaler's that afternoon."

I turned round and looked out of the front window of the car. It was no use. Ron Carpenter hadn't been in the square that day, hadn't seen his daughter when I had seen her.

"How did she find you?" Billy said. I had given up talking. I was imagining myself walking round a maze. Every time there seemed to be a way out I came to a dead-end.

"Through her mother. Lord, what a day that was, when Helen turned up in the shop. It was sheer luck that Sarah wasn't there. She's standing in front of me, cheeky as anything. Good-looking girl too. Just like her mother."

"Her mother?"

"A woman we knew from way back. It was a sleazy business, truth to tell, sneaking around. I don't know why I'm telling you all this anyway.

Annie, her name was, Annie Wilson. Funny thing was, we met through this support group, for childless married couples. Me and Sarah and Annie and her husband. Me and her just sort of hit it off. When she got pregnant it was obvious that it wasn't her husband's. They split up and Annie kept the baby. At least I thought she had. She never said anything, see, not to her husband – or to anyone – that I was the baby's father. That's how come Sarah never knew."

"Presumably Annie didn't keep the baby after all," Billy said.

"No, she was adopted at six months. Annie probably found it too hard-going, on her own with a small baby. Helen found her, I don't know how. She's living on the other side of London. Didn't want to know Helen apparently. She told her my name though and the address I'd previously been living at. It didn't take Helen long to find me here."

It was getting steamed up inside the car and I opened a window. I imagined Helen Driscoll walking the streets, searching for her natural father. Ron Carpenter continued. I noticed he kept his inhaler out, his finger cupped over it, ready for use.

"It got harder to keep it from Sarah because Helen started to get difficult. First couple of times she came to see me she was fine. I explained to her the circumstances, that Sarah couldn't know about her. But I said we could be friends. She could visit me occasionally, maybe go out. Sarah need never know, I said, and with all honesty she seemed to like that, thought it was fun." He was speaking faster and faster. "The trouble was, as the weeks went by, she started to come round more often; sometimes instead of going to school. I'd look out the window and see her sitting on the bench. Sometimes I'd slip out and talk to her but more and more I'd just have to ignore her. Truth to tell, it was very awkward."

It was *awkward*. I found myself looking at Ron Carpenter with growing dislike. He left his daughter sitting on a freezing cold bench because he was afraid to own up to his wife.

"And she started asking me to do things. She was having some problems with a previous boyfriend's father. He was threatening her, she said."

My ears pricked up at this; Billy looked around as well. Ron Carpenter looked startled to be the centre of our attention again.

"I shouldn't really be telling you this. I think I've said enough."

"Ron, please go on."

"I can't go to the police about any of this. I can't have any of it out in public. It would kill my wife."

"You don't have to go to the police, just tell us."

"She said her boyfriend's dad…"

"Inspector Martin," I said.

"Yes, that's him; she said he was threatening her. Something about getting her in trouble with the police for something that had happened with a car. I don't know. I said I'd see if I could speak to him. Thing is I often go to the police station. I deliver dry cleaning, you see. I've got a regular visitor's card. It's easy for me to see most of the officers who work down there."

"And did you see him? Inspector Martin?"

"I was going to. I was in the station the day after she told me but..."

"What?" Billy said.

"He was ... no, to be perfectly honest I got cold feet. If I had had a word with him, I'd have had to admit to being Helen's father. I was sure, I was positive it would get back to Sarah."

"So you didn't bother," I said. I couldn't keep the disdain out of my voice. He didn't seem to notice, just carried on.

"And then a few days later she was dead. I couldn't believe it. I didn't know what to think or feel. She was my daughter, true enough, but I didn't have any deep feelings for her. No more than for any other teenager..." Ron Carpenter held the inhaler up and sucked out of it. He sat, his lips tightly closed and looked from me to Billy and back again.

Billy started the car up; he had had enough.

"I mean if I had told Sarah, what good would it have done? Just upset her. And in the end, it would all have been for nothing. Poor Helen's dead."

We dropped him off at the end of the road. He

looked around again as he got out of the car. It was as if someone was following him. I watched him walk up the street and wondered how he could sleep at night. *Helen, you should have got to know me better.*

Maybe it was better that she hadn't.

Billy spoke first after we drove off.

"There was some trouble with a car," he said. "I don't remember seeing that in your notebook."

"No, it's the first time I've heard of it. Come to think of it, Fay Norris said something bad had happened down on a council estate. There was a party and it was when Helen and Roger had finished."

"So you need to talk to Roger again?"

"Oh, I don't know," I said, "maybe this is all a waste of time." I was tired. I wanted the whole thing to finish. Nothing was emerging from all the investigations; if anything, the story got more complicated every time we uncovered some new detail.

"You're not giving up now. Let's make this our last call. We'll talk to this Roger Martin and then tonight you can ring Heather Warren and wash your hands of the whole thing. If they don't think there's enough evidence to start the investigation, then it's no skin off your nose."

Billy was organizing me. I felt so grateful I could hardly speak.

"Where will Roger Martin be?" he asked.

"In school probably. Here, I've got the name of it under Helen's details. Westpark High."

"If we're quick, we might get there in time for the end of lessons."

18
The Party

Roger Martin came out of the school gate amid a stream of other kids, some running, some walking closely in twos, some, hands in pockets, whistling along the road. A few metres behind, running to keep up, was his girlfriend Suzy.

I was leaning against a shop opposite the gate of the school. As soon as Roger got free of the crowd of schoolkids I walked across to him. He saw me coming and smiled slowly. It was a controlled look. Suzy didn't smile, not at first. Her lips moved rapidly, saying something I couldn't hear. Then, as she came closely to me she smiled as well.

"Patsy," Roger said with a great show of pleasure, "is Brian around?" He looked up and down the street even though it was perfectly clear that I had been standing alone.

"Roger," I replied, "we need to talk about Helen Driscoll." I had decided to be completely straight with him.

"We've already talked about her. Anyway what's it to you?"

"I'm following up the case. There are some things that don't add up." I was overdosing on the clichés; any minute the words *the butler did it* were going to come out of my mouth.

"We told you everything about Helen, didn't we, Roger?" Suzy said, her arm linking Roger's.

"Not quite. You didn't tell me about the party or about the trouble with the car." I looked straight at Roger as I said this. He turned immediately to Suzy and said:

"You've told someone; I knew you couldn't keep your mouth shut."

"I never, Roger, I never said a word." Suzy was looking bewildered.

"Just keep quiet. That's all you had to do."

"Roger, I haven't…" Suzy had raised her voice. A number of younger kids were standing around us. Some of them were nudging each other.

Roger looked across me, out into the distance. He had shaken Suzy's arm away from his.

"What's it got to do with you? I don't have to talk to you about anything."

He looked so different from the first time we'd met. He'd been friendly, warm; now the joviality had gone; he was apprehensive, guarded.

"That's right, we don't have to talk to you, do we, Roger?" Suzy said, agreeing with him. I noticed her trying to slip her hand through his arm but he was holding his elbow flat against his side.

"Roger, last night I talked to Fay Norris who told me some things about Helen and you," I said. I took off my glasses and rubbed my nose. "I have a feeling that very soon the investigation over her death will be reopened. If you've got some secrets, then it would be better if you were to tell them before they come out by themselves."

I turned and started to walk away. I could see Billy, in the car, a few metres ahead on the other side of the road. After a few moments I heard footsteps.

"Wait, Patsy," Roger's voice came from behind, "I'll talk to you." Suzy was puffing a few metres behind him, her heels making it difficult for her to keep up.

"We'll talk to you, won't we, Roger," she said unnecessarily.

We went back to Billy's house. It was empty but after he had put his calor gas fire on it was warm. He put the kettle on and we all sat round the kitchen table.

"All of what I told you about Helen was true."

"It was," Suzy said.

"Shut up, Suze," Roger said and Suzy pursed her lips.

"She did harass us. She hated the idea of me and Suzy going out together."

"What about the car and the party. What happened there?"

"We'd been going downhill, her and me, rowing and stuff. I knew I was going to have to end it but it was difficult. She was always depressed and whenever I raised the subject she'd just start to cry."

Billy put the tea on the table and sat down.

"Fay Norris said that Helen knew Suzy was after you, had known for months; maybe that's why she was depressed."

"No," Roger said. He did look genuinely surprised. Suzy said nothing.

"Some kid from our class's parents were away. He was having a party. It was the end of last summer. We all went, most of the class. Helen was difficult all evening. She kept sniping at me, taking the mickey out of my dad. In the end I told her it was over. She started to drink, there was stuff around, I had some wine. Most of the kids from my class were gone by this time. Suzy had gone. There were only about five of us left."

Suzy was silently playing with her fingers, tapping them together, making shapes with them, a triangle, a circle, her palms together as if she was praying.

"Someone suggested that we went for a drive. Helen was all for it. She was loud by this time, very drunk. I wanted to go home but I didn't want to leave her there, on her own. Anyway the long and short of it was that we got into a car that was parked round the back of the estate. I thought, I honestly thought, that it belonged to one of the kids' brothers."

It was a stolen car. Roger Martin had got into a *stolen* car.

"Everyone took a turn to drive, just up and down the road. It was pitch dark, you know the road that leads down to the river, where all the empty houses are. We weren't doing any harm, no speeding, no messing around, no hand-brake turns or anything stupid like that."

"But you'd been drinking," Billy said.

"Yes." Roger stopped speaking.

"They'd all had more than you, hadn't they, Roger. He was the most sober," Suzy said.

"That's true. That was the trouble. If I had been really drunk I'd just have done what the others did and left the car down by the river. Trouble was I was still thinking it belonged to one of their brothers. I wasn't drunk but Helen was. She was lying across the back seat. I decided to return the car to where we'd got it from. I don't know why I did it. I could have just left it there and no one would have ever known."

Roger Martin had his eyes closed and his hands were shaped into fists.

"What happened?" Billy asked.

"I drove it back towards the flats. Helen was awake by this time. She kept saying 'don't leave me, Roger, don't go'. I must have looked round into the back seat or something because somehow I lost control. There was this cat, see, in front of me. It hadn't been there before. All I saw were these eyes in the headlights of the car and I swerved to avoid them. I don't know why I didn't just brake, maybe I did, but whatever, the car crashed into this other car that was parked at the side of the road. It made a massive bang and then there was this even bigger silence."

"Didn't you get hurt?" Billy said.

"I had a seat-belt on. Like I said we weren't joy-riding. I was taking the car back."

"Returning it," Suzy said, her voice shaky.

"And?" I was impatient to hear the rest.

"I got out of the car. I pulled Helen out and we ran. I just panicked. I just ran until we got home. My dad was there. I don't remember much. I think I might have even been crying. I just remember not knowing what to do and then he was there and he took it over."

"He covered it up?" I said, surprised, remembering the stern photograph of him in the newspaper.

Roger said nothing, he just shook his head from side to side.

"If only I'd just left the car down by the river."

"Nobody lost out of it," said Suzy. "The car owners will have got their insurance and it's not as if anyone was hurt."

"For a while Helen was quiet about it. Like I said, after we first broke up she seemed OK, really quite aloof, like she didn't care. I saw her a couple of times, on her own."

"You never said," Suzy said, looking down at the table.

"She was quite pleasant. Mentioned the crash once or twice, but it was like, 'thank God we got out of that, I'll never be able to thank your dad for keeping us out of trouble,' and then one day, like overnight, she just changed."

I thought about Joe Driscoll's words: *I sorted her out*. He had. The revelation of her having been adopted had changed her character.

"She came to me and said she wanted to go out with me again. Then she would keep her mouth shut about the crash. She said she would go to the police station and say what had happened. It would have been the end for my dad and for me. I'd never have got a job in the force then." He sounded much more concerned for himself than for his dad.

"He'd have lost his career just for one little mistake," Suzy said.

"My dad said he would warn her off. He did. He went to see her about a week before she died. I don't know what was said but he told me it would be OK, that he had sorted it out. He said he'd told her about the trouble she'd get into if she said anything. In the end, none of that really matters because she died anyway."

"We were shocked, weren't we, Roger?" Suzy seemed to feel a need to say.

"No, no, not shocked. I was relieved and that's the truth."

"No," Suzy said.

"Shut up, Suze."

It was quiet in the room and in my head I kept thinking of Inspector Martin; a troublesome girl on his hands, a series of murders that were being followed up by his colleagues. What if there was one more, would it matter? If he made it look like all the others?

Roger and Suzy sat for a while talking. Then they went out into the dark night. As they walked up the path I could hear his voice, flat and dull; over the top, high-pitched, I could hear Suzy's words: "Won't we, Roger, shouldn't we, Roger, doesn't it, Roger."

Roger seemed shell-shocked by all of it. I wondered how he would feel if he thought that his dad had murdered Helen Driscoll in order to keep himself and his son in a job.

I went back into Billy's kitchen.

"I'm going to do what you said."

"Really?" he smiled, rinsing the cups under the tap.

"I'm going to unload all of it on to Heather Warren. She can deal with Inspector Martin."

Billy came towards me, drying the cups with a tea towel.

"Take care, Patsy," he said. "It's an awful big jump, from being a decent police officer to a murderer. There's no real evidence that it was him."

Billy was being cautious again.

"I know, I know, but he's got the motive and the means. Think about it; this police inspector's under-age son drives a stolen car while under the influence of drink and then crashes it. This police inspector covers it up, allowing his son to get off scot-free. If it had come out it would have cost him his career, not to mention his son's. Helen Driscoll certainly had a wild, unbalanced side to her. Perhaps he tried to keep her quiet but in the end she kept on. Look how she found her mum and plagued her dad. She could be relentless. Perhaps, in the end, he couldn't stand it any more."

"OK, perhaps," Billy said. "Just be careful when you're talking to Heather."

"I will," I said.

19
The Wrong Man

Heather listened in silence while I spoke. There was no expression on her face as I described my visit to Fay Norris and my discovery of Helen Driscoll's natural father. I had my notebook on my lap and my voice was racing with excitement. As I went on though I could see there was no surprise or astonishment in her eyes about my findings, my revelations or my solution.

I had had to get her out of a meeting, had told her my information was urgent.

"It had better be," she'd said testily as she led me up to her office. As she listened I noticed the absence of cigarettes. In her hands she had a pencil that she kept playing with, weaving it in and out of her fingers, tapping it lightly on the desk in front of her, holding it up in the air, the end of it in her mouth like an imaginary pipe.

At the mention of Inspector Martin she seemed visibly to stiffen. She put the pencil down and picked up a small Plexiglas ruler which she proceeded to bend and then straighten. I began to feel like a naughty schoolgirl, summoned to the Head's office, trying to explain away my rôle in some major school mischief. When I'd finished I sat waiting for a few seconds. My throat seemed full of something that I couldn't swallow.

There was a knock on the door and a young man came in.

"Excuse me, marm, but your car is ready."

"Thanks, John," Heather said and started to gather things off her desk into an attaché case. When the door had shut behind the young man she said:

"Patsy, when you and I spoke the other night we made a deal. That deal was that I would find out about alibis and you would drop this investigation. You agreed to that, right?"

I nodded glumly. She was angry with me.

"Now I find you haven't kept your side of the bargain, that you're still meddling in it all, poking your nose into the lives of the people I work with."

I listened with a sinking heart. *Poking your nose.* The words stung me.

The interview hadn't gone the way I had hoped it would. I think I had imagined myself being the centre of a lot of back-slapping. *Well done, Patsy* was the phrase I had thought might be directed at me. Instead I was being treated like a first-year who had been caught smoking behind the gym.

I began to feel angry with Heather. I said nothing though, I let her speak on. She was standing up pulling paper and files together, talking to me at the same time, no eye contact, just a steely edge to her voice.

"For your information, Patsy, John Martin did come to me at the time that his son crashed the car. He did not, as you put it, *cover it up*, he came and told me exactly what had happened, not quite as graphically as you just have. I, personally, followed it up. John Martin is a valued colleague here. I felt I owed it to him to try and help when he was in trouble.

"The car in question had been stolen, some months before. It was an old car that the insurers had written off and sent to the breaker's yard for spare parts. One of the boys from the estate had presumably stolen it from there."

My redrafted notes were lying on my lap. I turned a page and saw line after line of slanted blue handwriting. I'd even underlined some things. I almost laughed out loud. How important I'd thought I was.

"The car he crashed into was a derelict car. It hadn't even got any wheels, had been parked in that spot for weeks." She clicked her attaché case shut. She went to a coat stand and took a silk scarf and wrapped it round her neck.

"Theoretically you're right. John Martin's son did break the law but you know, Patsy, sometimes you have to give a little. No one had been hurt, no one had lost money. If we had charged Roger Martin all that would have happened is that he would have received a caution or, at the very most, if it had gone to magistrates, some community service. I, myself, felt sure that he would never offend again. The end result would have been that a young man who had wanted to be a policeman all his life wouldn't have been able to join.

"I took a decision. I think it was the right one."

"But Helen Driscoll was trying to blackmail Inspector Martin..." I said weakly.

"But she had nothing to blackmail him with! The case was closed, and anyway," she was buttoning up her coat, "even if what you're saying is right and John Martin did have a motive for murdering Helen Driscoll, he has an alibi. In fact John Martin has an alibi for the whole of that afternoon. He was with me. We were at a liaison conference. We were sitting with one of the members from the local council when my bleeper went off and I was informed that my officers were chasing a suspect down along the railway. We both left the meeting and were there, minutes later, when Knight was caught. He was beside me, Patsy, so he couldn't have murdered anyone."

She stood by the door, stiff and formal. Misery must have been written all over my face because after a few moments she softened and put her case on the floor. She came across and sat on the edge of the desk.

"Don't think I'm not impressed with your determination, Patsy, but you've got to stop playing at this. If you want to be a real detective, come and join the force; otherwise you're just playing around in the dark, embarrassing yourself and other people. You'll end up a laughing stock. I don't know what your uncle would think."

She looked at her watch and got up to go. I stood up and looking through the windows of her office I could see the CID detectives milling around in the room outside. There were one or two faces I thought I recognized and over by one of the computer monitors was Des Murray's back. As I walked out they were all looking away, at bits of paper or thumbing through files, and one or two were on the phone. Even the cleaning woman seemed to turn away from me. I turned and walked to the door and felt every pair of eyes on my back, boring into me; they all knew I had messed up, every one of them.

It was dark and cold outside and I pulled my collar

up and the woolly brim of my hat down. This case had been like a Russian doll. Every time I had lifted one off there had been another underneath; one solution had led to another set of problems.

Inspector Martin had been with Heather.

I should have listened to Billy Rogers.

My mum was in and so was her friend Sheila. They were both sitting on the settee, in front of the TV, eating an Indian takeaway meal.

"There's some chicken biryani in the fridge for you," my mum said in between mouthfuls. "Put it in the microwave."

I went to the kitchen and took the food out of the fridge even though I wasn't very hungry. I didn't fancy joining my mum and Sheila. Sheila was bound to make some comment about the murders or Leslie Knight and it was the last thing I wanted to talk about. I tipped the food on to a plate and slid it into the microwave.

Just then the doorbell rang and I shouted, "I'll get it," and went to the front door. It was Brian Martin.

"Brian!" I said. In all the rush and hurry to go and see Heather Warren I'd completely forgotten about Brian. No doubt his brother had told him all the things I'd said.

"Can I come in?" His face was long. "I won't be long. I'm not stopping."

I took him into the kitchen. The buzzer sounded in the microwave but I left my food there.

"A cup of tea?" I said lightly, nervously. I had a feeling that I was about to be told off again. Twice in one day; I was getting used to it.

He ignored my offer.

"Why didn't you tell me you were investigating Helen Driscoll's death?"

"I wasn't really," I said, still lying. I looked at Brian Martin's face. His expression had a hard edge to it. I'd been unfair to him. I should have told him the truth.

"You used me," he said, as if reading my thoughts. "You could have been honest with me. I wouldn't have minded you talking to Roger. If he'd had anything to do with Helen's death, then I'd have wanted to find out the truth."

"I'm sorry," I said. "It did start off that way, me wanting to find out about your brother and Helen but…" I was stumbling for words, "but I really did get to like you."

It was weak even though it was true.

"It's all right; you don't have to be nice to me any more. You don't need any more information."

"Brian, I'm…" I put my hand on to his arm but he shook it off.

"You could have been honest. Maybe I could actually have helped you."

"I'm sorry." It was all I could say. He was right. If

I had been honest from the start, then maybe the misunderstandings, the mysteries, would have been cleared up more quickly.

"You weren't really interested in the truth," he said, "you just wanted to be the hero."

The door opened and my mum came in carrying two empty plates. I could hear the TV from the other room.

"Sorry, Pat. I didn't know you had company."

"She hasn't," Brian said. "I'm just off."

I walked to the front door with a dozen things to say rushing round my head. I never got the chance though; he opened the door and went through it without so much as a backward glance. I stood looking out into the dark as his back disappeared into the night.

Even though I hadn't really wanted him I felt as if I'd lost something. I leant up against the door jamb, weary with the whole thing. *You just wanted to be the hero ... you weren't really interested in the truth.* The words settled in my head like lead.

"Your food's ready, Pat," I could hear my mum's voice.

"I don't want it," I said and walked off upstairs.

20
The Letter

I got up on Wednesday morning feeling as though I had a bad hangover, even though I'd had nothing to drink.

You just wanted to be the hero were the first words that came into my head when my alarm woke me up. I also remembered Billy's cutting words: *you want all the glory; you want to be the centre of attention again...*

Was it true? Had I been more interested in my own position than in solving the case?

As I was getting dressed I told myself that it hadn't been like that. My tights got twisted though and the zip stuck on my jeans; a button came off my shirt and the jumper I wanted to wear was in a crumpled heap on the floor from the previous day. Frustration was simmering inside me and when I couldn't find the scarf I wanted I slammed the wardrobe door shut and broke the magnetic catch.

The door swung idly back and hung dismally open.

It wasn't going to be my day.

My mum handed me a letter when I got downstairs. It was a large brown envelope with my name and address written in block letters on the front. I picked up the mug of tea she'd made me and sat down at the table. Inside was another smaller envelope addressed to Fay Norris in Bethnal Green. There was a note with it. It read:

To Patsy Kelly. I got this in the post yesterday with a note from Helen's mum, Mrs Driscoll. She said she'd found it in among Helen's things. It had been stuck down and was ready to send so she thought it was probably private and forwarded it to me.

Helen must have written it on the day that she died, meaning to post it to me. I thought, after the things you said, that you might be interested in it.

Poor Helen, she wasn't all bad. I wish I'd been kinder to her now. Fay.

My mum was making the breakfast and talking about her day at college. I said "um" a couple of times and opened the letter from Helen Driscoll, dated the tenth of January.

Dear Fay, I haven't been over for a while because I've been busy trying to find my real mum and dad. I spent some time looking through my mum and dad's papers and found some information on a group they used to belong to, Childless Couples Support Association. It seems they used to go there regularly before I was born. While they were there, they heard of a woman who had a baby she couldn't look after. Me!! They have a letter from this woman, Annie, her name is. There was an address on it and I went there and got a forwarding address. Annie, my real mum, lives in north London now. I went to see her a couple of weeks ago. She is so nice. There's a problem; her present husband doesn't know about me, so we're not going to see each other for a while until she tells him. It's only fair that I give her some time. The other good thing is that she gave me the address of my real dad! I've been to see him; he works in a dry cleaner's in a local precinct here. We've had a few chats, he's really nice, although a bit nervous about his wife finding out. I've kept going to see him though. He likes me a lot, I think. His wife's a bit unstable apparently. She's had some kind of breakdown and has been in hospital.

Today though I got a big surprise. He sent me a letter asking me to meet him at two-thirty in the square. He wants to tell his wife about me so that it's all out in the open. It'll be great. In a few months my real mum will have told her husband, then I'll have all sorts of relatives!

By the way, I'm getting on better with Mum and Dad at home; even daft Joe isn't annoying me so much now. I even saw Roger Martin the other day, with his puppy dog Suzy, and for the first time I didn't feel like crying.

Things are looking up for me. See you soon. Love and kisses. Helen.

I put the letter down on the table. In front of me was a mug of tea and a plate of toast that my mum must have put there while I had been reading. I found myself breathing very shallowly.

Helen Driscoll's father had arranged to see her on the afternoon of the tenth of January. That's why she'd been sitting there, on the bench. She'd been waiting to meet him.

I remembered him hurrying after me and Billy as we'd left the dry cleaner's: *she says she's my daughter. That I'm her father, that I was her father.*

He'd said nothing to us about having arranged to meet his daughter that afternoon, not a word. I sat with my head in my hands and tried to think back over the conversation. I'd taken no notes. I'd only picked up on the stuff about Helen being threatened by Inspector Martin. I'd not really held on to what he'd said at all.

Phrases kept coming back to me; no, to be perfectly honest, in all honesty, truth to tell. He was constantly emphasizing the fact that he was telling the truth. But he'd said nothing about meeting Helen on the tenth of January.

I got up and walked around the room. I heard the radio on upstairs and the sound of the shower running. I picked up a bit of cold toast and nibbled at it.

I went through it all, trying to imagine what might have happened.

Ron Carpenter and his wife Sarah couldn't have children. They met another couple at a support group and Ron had an affair with the woman, Annie. Helen was born although no one knew about it. Annie moved away; eventually Helen was adopted by Mr and Mrs Driscoll.

Helen was fifteen and had found her real mum and dad. Neither of them seemed to want to know her. She left her mum alone but continued to approach her dad, not realizing (or maybe ignoring) the fact that he wasn't very keen to take her into his life.

He was desperate that his wife shouldn't find out but Helen continued to sit out in the square, a ghost from his past.

Ron Carpenter worked for a dry cleaning company. He had a contract with the local police station to launder and clean uniforms. He had a regular pass there, delivering stuff that he had cleaned. The newspapers were full of the Railway Murders. At the station Ron overheard or even saw the information about Operation Rose. Because he was not closely involved he didn't get all the information; he only knew that a rose was left on the bodies, not what colour it was.

Helen continued to plague him and he was terrified that his wife Sarah would find out. He had no real feelings for the girl; he had said so, to me and to Billy. He asked her to meet him at two-thirty, perhaps took her away, in his van, to a deserted railway yard. In the back of his van he had a piece of climbing rope and a single yellow rose.

I was eating my toast as though it was a piece of chewing gum. I let it go and swallowed.

What could I do about it?

I could hardly go to Heather Warren, not after what she had said to me.

I couldn't just leave it though.

I would have to go and see Ron Carpenter.

21
Yellow Roses

I found Billy at home. He was in his overalls, getting ready to start work on a car he was servicing for a man down the road.

I showed him the letter and brought him up to date on my meeting with Heather Warren. I half expected him to try and talk me out of going to see Ron Carpenter, to suggest some other course of action. He didn't though. He got changed into his jeans and a jacket. On his way out of the front door he picked up a large spanner and put it into his jacket pocket.

It was only eight-thirty when we got there. The shop was closed. We rang the bell for three or four minutes. I looked around the square while I was waiting. The newspaper hoarding outside the Asian shop said: "RAILWAY MURDERS: *Psychologist comments on mind of serial killers.*" It was just over a week since Helen Driscoll had been murdered and yet Leslie Knight was still making the headlines.

Eventually we started to knock on the glass, looking through into the interior of the shop before Ron Carpenter appeared. He came forward with a quizzical expression on his face and unbolted the door at the top and bottom; then turning the key, he opened it.

"What's going on?" he said, looking at his watch. "We're not open yet."

He stopped for a minute, looking closely at us. Then he said:

"You're the two I spoke to the other day about Helen. What do you want? It's lucky my Sarah's out. What do you want?"

"Can we come in, Mr Carpenter? I've got something very important I want to say to you about Helen."

Ron Carpenter looked cross. He looked out into the square, as if to see whether anyone was watching.

"You better come up then," he said grudgingly.

The flat upstairs was tiny. The three of us walked single file along a narrow hallway into a small living room. There was a settee and an easy-chair with several cushions scattered about. On the far wall were a number of framed photographs, all of groups of adults.

"Where's your wife?" Billy asked.

"She works part-time, cleaning," Ron Carpenter said. "What's all this about?"

It was while looking round that I saw the bowl of yellow roses.

I walked across to it. It was one of those crystal glass bowls that had a steel mesh fitting across it so that the roses could stand up separately. I put my finger out to one of the blooms and the petals came off at my touch and floated down to the table top, where they joined several others. The flowers had been there for some time.

There was something unsettling about the roses being there. It gave me a shiver. Had Ron Carpenter bought a bunch of roses, selected one for his purpose and saved the rest as a gift for his fragile, over-protected wife?

Billy looked over at me and the roses and walked towards the door. He had his hand inside his jacket. I wondered if he thought we were going to need a weapon.

"What is this? What's going on?" Ron Carpenter said.

I decided to be blunt, more for shock value than for anything else.

"Did you kill your daughter, Ron?"

His mouth fell open and he took a step back as if the very sentence had knocked him from his spot.

"What do you mean?" he said. He pushed his

hand deep into his pocket and came out with his inhaler. He held it by the side of his face and looked at me with apprehension.

"We think that Helen was murdered by someone who wanted her out of the way; to stop her being a nuisance."

"But she was killed by that, that madman, that bloke they caught!" He was looking aghast. He put out his arm and leant on the back of a chair.

"No she wasn't. I have a letter here, in my pocket, that she wrote to her friend on the day she died. She said you had asked her to meet you, at two-thirty. She said you were going to tell your wife about her."

At each thing I said, he seemed to grow weaker. I looked across at Billy. He had his arm across the door as if he was expecting Ron Carpenter to make a run for it. The way he was standing, the expression on his face, it didn't look as though he could make a run for the settee, let alone for anything else. A tiny doubt began to take root in my head.

"You wanted her out of the way, Ron. You didn't want your wife to know about her. She wouldn't go away though, would she? Every time you looked out of the window she was sitting there in the middle of the square staring across at you."

He put the inhaler into his mouth but didn't use it. I walked across the room to the wall that was full of photos.

"No, I was ... cross at her ... but –" the words

came out of Ron Carpenter's mouth as if he was speaking in a foreign tongue and searching for the right vocabulary – "my wife ... she..."

My attention was taken by a photo on the wall of a woman in an overall in the middle of a group of men, one of whom I recognized. It was Des Murray, the CID officer I had spent the day with. I was still talking to Ron but part of my mind was wondering why Des's photo should be there.

"You had access to the police station and could have found out about the roses that the murderer had left on the bodies of the other victims. It was easy for you to make it look like it was the work of the Railway Killer."

Then I realized where the photo had been taken. It was in the CID room and some of the other male faces looked familiar. The woman even began to look like someone I knew. It was Ron Carpenter's wife, Sarah, who had been behind the counter on the day we'd come into the shop. She looked different in the photo, her hair tightly pulled back from her face.

"You bought roses, even though they were the wrong colour, Ron," I could hear Billy's voice finishing off the line of questioning.

I looked round at Ron, suddenly sure that we'd made a mistake. He was ashen, rubbing his hands together.

"Truth to tell," he said, "I didn't buy those roses;

my Sarah did."

"My God," I said, "your wife bought the roses."

I had a flashback to the day I had seen Helen in the square. I was looking over my shoulder at the shops behind me and I saw Majestic Dry Cleaner's. Inside there was a woman peering out through the glass. Helen was watching the shop but it was a *woman* looking out, a *woman* who had made the appointment to see Helen, not a man.

"Where is Sarah, Ron?" I almost shouted at him.

"She's at work, at the police station. Why?"

I walked swiftly past him, down the stairs and out of the flat.

When I got to the station I asked to see Heather. She wasn't available, was actually in a meeting with my uncle Tony. Stevie came down to the front desk.

"Patsy!" she said, when she saw me. "How have you been?"

"Fine, fine. This is my friend Billy Rogers," I said impatiently, pointing behind me. "Stevie, we need to come upstairs…" She was screwing her mouth up. I went on: "We desperately need to see my uncle Tony. I've got some important stuff to tell him. I've got to do it personally. Heather won't mind."

She looked unsure but she got a couple of visitors' badges out anyway. We followed her through the entrance and into the building.

When we got up to the CID suite I saw Sarah Carpenter immediately. She was polishing some of the desktops down at the far end of the office. She was the cleaner who had helped me mop up my spilt tea on the day I'd spent with CID. She looked different from when she'd been behind the counter in the dry cleaner's, less hot and bothered, her hair neatly tied back.

Walking through the long room, Billy behind me, I was aware of people stopping their work to look at us. Through the glass I could see Heather's face although it was clear that she hadn't seen me. She looked as if she was deep in conversation with my uncle. I could see the back of his head, nodding at something she had said.

I walked up to the woman and said:

"Sarah, remember me? I came into the shop the other day and asked you about Helen Driscoll."

Stevie was alongside me.

"What's going on?" she said, touching my elbow.

Sarah Carpenter had stopped cleaning, had put her duster and spray can down on the desk. She looked at me straight, eye to eye.

"Sarah," I said softly, "did you arrange to meet Helen on the afternoon she was killed?"

The office was going quiet. From behind I could hear whispers and the sound of a door opening. Heather Warren's voice came from far away.

Still Sarah Carpenter said nothing, just gave me

an unblinking stare.

"Did you buy the yellow roses, Sarah? Did you kill Helen?"

"What on earth?" Stevie said. I could hear Heather's voice, crossly: *What's going on?* and my uncle Tony: *Patricia, what's happening, have you gone mad?*

"Did you kill her, Sarah? And leave the yellow rose behind to make it look like the Railway Killer?"

Sarah Carpenter sat down slowly. The chair she chose was a swivel one and she had to steady herself by leaning on the desk. She mumbled something that I couldn't quite hear.

"What, Sarah, what did you say?" I said, holding my breath. The tension in the room was so strong you could have stopped a train with it.

"She was going to take him away, like her mother tried to. Every day I watched her sitting in the square, looking into the shop, trying to catch his eye. He thought I didn't know, but I'd always known. Annie Wilson had told me about the baby. I just dared her to try and take my Ronnie away. The daughter, the dead one, I'd have known her anywhere. She was the spitting image of her mother; tiny, skinny. A puff of wind would have blown her away. I knew it was her. I'd been waiting for her for years…"

"Sarah," Heather said, "do you know what you're saying?"

"I know. I know what I've done. Don't think I could ever forget it."

I heard a male voice from behind me.

"I think you should read her her rights, marm." It was Des Murray.

Heather looked flustered. After a moment she started in a calm voice:

"You do not have to say anything, but anything you do say…"

I turned and, pulling the sleeve of Billy's jacket, started to walk out of the room.

My uncle Tony's head was turning back and forth, looking from me to Heather and back again.

"Let's get out of here," I said.

22
Copycat

The newspapers were full of it.
"*RAILWAY KILLER'S LAST VICTIM KILLED BY JEALOUS WIFE*" – and – "*COPYCAT MURDER IN BID TO FOOL POLICE*".

Heather Warren was quoted extensively:

"*We became aware, as the days went by, that the evidence and facts in the Driscoll death were not exactly the same as those in the previous murders. It was important to keep our investigations secret as we realized that only someone with a link to the station could have broken the security of Operation Rose and concocted such a scheme. We did, in fact, have help from the public on this case.*"

I was sitting on the floor of Billy's living room

with the newspapers spread out in front of me. Billy was on a chair just behind me. Every few minutes I leaned back and felt his knees poking into my shoulder blades.

"There's not a mention of me anywhere!" I said, making a small pile of the newspapers that we'd bought.

"Not that you're worried," Billy said, reaching across and picking up one of the papers. "It's not as if you wanted to be the hero or anything."

"No," I said. His mention of the word *hero* made me thing of Brian Martin. I'd seen him just the previous day. He'd been coming out of PHOTO-KWIK as I'd been passing. I'd started to smile at him, determined to make friends again, but he'd steadfastly ignored me and walked on as if I wasn't there. I'd felt a pang of something; whether it was guilt or loss I couldn't have said.

"What I don't see is how Sarah Carpenter got Helen Driscoll to go to the railway warehouses with her," Billy said.

"Oh, Heather told me," I said. "Apparently Sarah met Helen, probably just minutes after I'd left the square, and said that Ron was making deliveries and had broken down. She told her that they'd go and pick him up and then they could have their talk about the future. She was very pleasant and chatty to Helen; she must have been, to put her at her ease. Helen probably didn't even notice where they were going until it was too late."

I felt a little shiver saying that. At what point had it become *too late*? When she'd got into the car? When she'd got out of the car and walked into the warehouse? Or when she'd first found her dad and sat in the square, watched by Sarah Carpenter?

I leaned back, my neck aching from bending over. I could feel Billy's knees behind me.

"Here," he said, and put his hands on my shoulders and started to rub them. I closed my eyes and felt my shoulders relax and the muscles in my neck soften.

"That's good," I said and I thought, for the five hundredth time, about the kiss we had had and not mentioned. We were like partners in a medieval dance, coming together and then pulling apart; a little twirl here and a curtsy there, now and then a touching of the hands.

It was frustrating.

"So, Detective Kelly," he said softly, "what are you going to investigate next?"

I turned round to look up at him. "I'll think of something," I said.

Look out for Patsy's next case…

PATSY KELLY INVESTIGATES

No Through Road

It was at about six o'clock that evening that the news of the dead boy came through. My mum and I were in the kitchen toasting some bread when Gerry Lawrence arrived. My mum bounced down the hall to open the door for him. I could hear them murmuring as they came back into the room. Gerry looked different from usual, his face grim, his mouth in a straight line. He took his glasses off.

"Something terrible's happened, Patsy," my mum said. "One of the boys from Gerry's group has been killed on the Link Road site."

Gerry plonked down on to the chair. He seemed to have doubled in weight and without his glasses his eyes had sunk back into his head.

"What happened?" I said, pulling a chair out to sit down on.

Gerry shook his head from side to side. He honestly looked as though he was on the brink of tears.

"One of the boys from the Fresh Air Campaign, Eddie Wolf. He was only seventeen and he's dead," my mum said, putting her fingers into Gerry's hair and stroking it.

"I know his dad!" Gerry said with emotion in his voice. "And his mum."

The details came out on the local news the next day. Most of them I'd already got, in bits and pieces from Gerry. Billy had even rung me up mid evening and told me a couple of things he'd heard down at his local pub.

Eddie Wolf had been one of the protesters; he'd been involved in some of the demonstrations in the previous weeks. He'd been one of the kids who had chained himself to one of the big trees on the common that was being knocked down to make way for the road. He was meant to take part in the demonstration on Easter Monday, the one that Billy and me saw from the pub garden, but he hadn't turned up.

After they had left us the protesters had walked slowly up by the wooden fences that cordoned the whole area off. There'd been a plan hatched before, apparently, that on a certain signal they'd all stop singing and make a run for the main gate, fling it

open and run into the site, jumping on the equip-
ment, chaining or tying themselves to it.

It took the police and the security men by
surprise. The gates fell back against the crowd and
once they were in they all ran towards the
machinery.

There was three or four minutes of noise and
scuffle until a loud scream stopped everyone. A
young woman was found, standing opposite a giant
cement mixer. She was stock still as though stuck to
the spot, her mouth wide open.

Eddie Wolf's face was visible, a ghastly bluish
colour. It was as if he was peeking out of the mixer,
except that he was still and stiff, not unlike the
hardened cement that was holding him there. The
fire brigade had had to cut him out of the cement
mixer. Even then, his body was still half encased in
concrete. He had to be taken, like that, in a van to
the morgue where the pathologists had to chip off
the remaining stuff.

I could just imagine them: men in white coats,
tiny hammers and chisels in their hands, their
foreheads creased in concentration. They must
have looked like artists, sculpting the form of a boy.

A lifeless boy who would never move again.

It gave me a bad feeling.

P●INT CRiME

A murder has been committed . . . Whodunnit?
Was it the teacher, the schoolgirl, or the best friend? An exciting series of crime novels, with tortuous plots and lots of suspects, designed to keep the reader guessing till the very last page.

Kiss of Death
School for Death
Peter Beere

Avenging Angel
Break Point
Final Cut
Shoot the Teacher
The Beat:
Missing Person
Black and Blue
Devid Belbin

Baa Baa Dead Sheep
Jill Bennett

A Dramatic Death
Margaret Bingley

Driven to Death
Patsy Kelly Investigates:
A Family Affair
Anne Cassidy

Overkill
Alane Ferguson

Deadly Music
Death Penalty
Dennis Hamley

Concrete Evidence
The Smoking Gun
Malcolm Rose

Dance With Death
Jean Ure

Look out for:
Deadly Inheritance
David Belbin

The Beat:
Smokescreen
David Belbin

The Alibi
Malcolm Rose

Follow six student nurses as they come to terms with doctors, patients, study ... and each other.

NURSES

Bette Paul

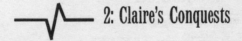

1: Katie Goes to College

Katie wants to get involved in *everything* when she starts at nursing college. But has she bitten off more than she can chew?

2: Claire's Conquests

Claire's finding nursing harder than she expected. And she's having problems with her love-life, too...

Look out for:

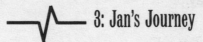

3: Jan's Journey

Can Jan's new life at St Ag's Hospital help him forget the horrors of his past?

Point

Pointing the way forward

More compelling reading from top authors.

Flight 116 is Down
Forbidden
Unforgettable
Caroline B. Cooney

Someone Else's Baby
Geraldine Kaye

Hostilities
Caroline Macdonald

I Carried You On Eagles' Wings
Sue Mayfield

Seventeenth Summer
K.M. Peyton

The Highest Form of Killing
Son of Pete Flude
Malcolm Rose

Secret Lives
William Taylor